ARATON

DARK WARRIOR ALLIANCE BOOK 22

BRENDA TRIM

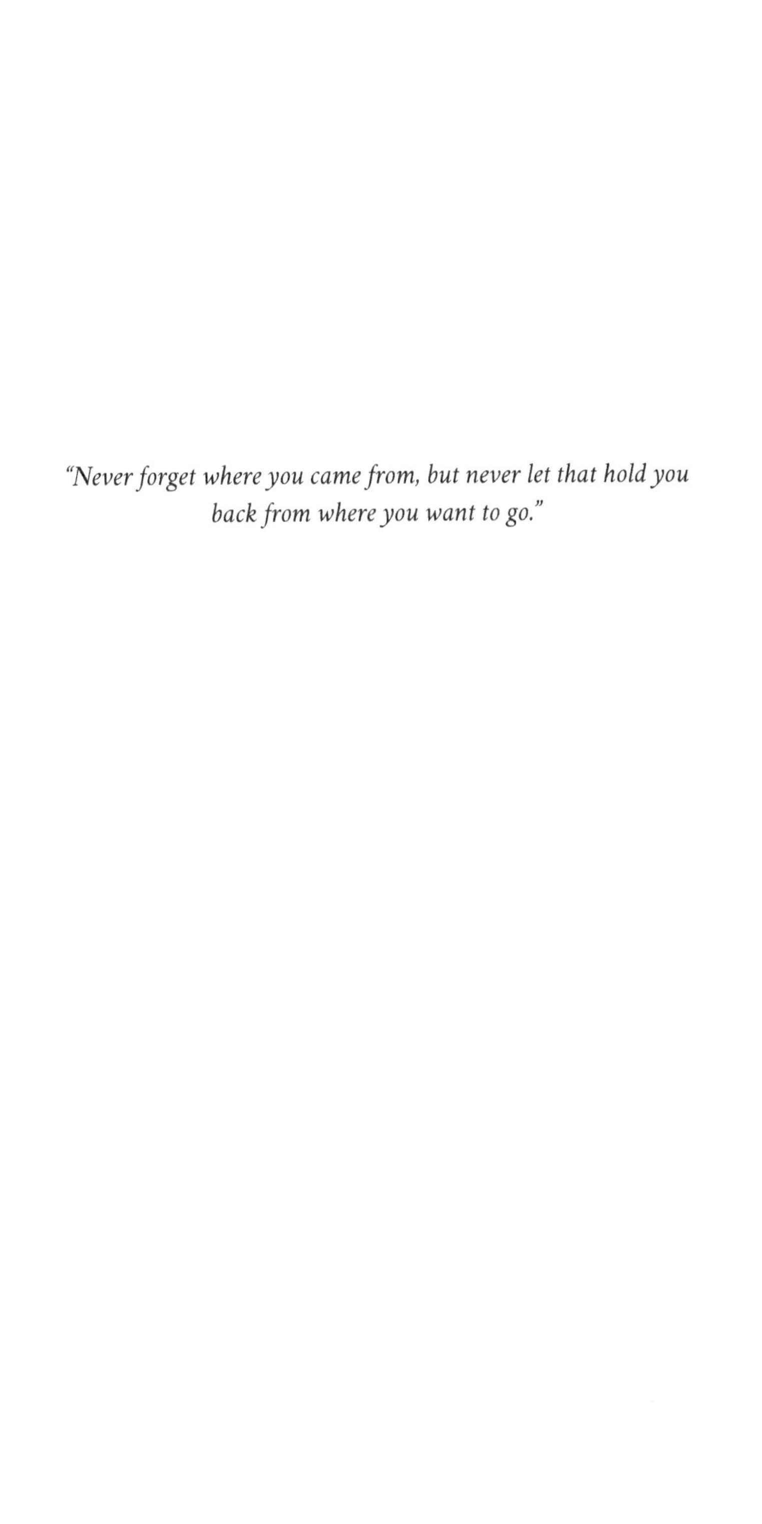

*"Never forget where you came from, but never let that hold you
back from where you want to go."*

CHAPTER 1

"Why the hell do they always pick this house to have their weird rituals around?" Lia asked her partner rhetorically.

The LaLaurie mansion on Royal Street was a cop's worst nightmare and a tourist's dream. People from all over the world came to New Orleans for many reasons. And Lia swore ninety percent of those that visited her city eventually hoofed it one block from Bourbon Street over to the corner of Royal and Governor Nicholls.

Most were drunk as she and Ben, her partner on the New Orleans Police force discovered when they climbed out of their patrol car. A native of NOLA, Natalia grew up on ghost stories and accounts of the hauntings at the LaLaurie mansion.

The origin of these stemmed from the tragic events that caused the hauntings in the first place. Depending on who you talked to, the original owner of this massive home was a demon disguised as a woman. Delphine LaLaurie.

Madame LaLaurie as she was known later in her life was recognized as a Creole socialite and serial killer. The accusations of torture and murder continue to this day almost two hundred years later. Natalia had no doubt the woman was pure evil. The stories existed for a reason, after all.

It is said that she broke the bones of some slaves and set them to heal at odd angles so that the women looked like a crab. Reports of hearing scratching steps are numerous.

Other stories involved her skinning her victims alive. There are accounts of the gruesome sight of slaves with their muscle and bone exposed while they gasp for breath and pray for death. And, stories get worse about her drilling holes in their skulls. Whatever the truth, there was a whole lotta nasty mojo in the house and earth beneath.

Yeah, natives of New Orleans believed in all sorts of paranormal mumbo jumbo like the soil being tainted. There were rituals most performed when they purchased a house to cleanse the area of malevolent energy.

"What I want to know is why there are still so many people out on the streets," Ben added as they started down the street toward the house in question.

That was a good point. There was a pandemic taking over the world at the moment. A virus, COVID-19, had appeared a couple months ago across the globe and in a few short weeks had spread to nearly every country on earth.

Natalia had never seen anything like it. What started like a common cold with a fever and coughing was claiming thousands of lives everywhere. Doctors and hospitals couldn't keep up with new cases thanks to the disease transmitting at break-neck speed. Like a freight train that lost its brakes and keeps barreling down the tracks despite the numerous cars placed in its way.

As a result of the virus most areas in the country have issued a shelter in place order asking people to stay at home to stop the spread of the disease. There was no way the group congregated around the mansion were all essential workers.

Guiding a ghost tour of the French Quarter was by no means a necessary service. The restaurants and bars were closed to patrons, but they did have order pickup available. This shit was never going away unless people started to listen and stay the fuck at home.

COVID-19 was no joke. It was killing more people than the flu did every year in a matter of weeks. Lia wasn't taking a chance with getting sick. Police were needed now more than ever with vandalism, fighting and various other crimes on the rise. Being cooped up would do that to a person.

Tugging her face mask over her mouth and nose, Lia slipped her leather gloves on before she reached the crowd. As they got closer, she realized this was a small crowd for the quarter.

Especially when you consider people were wall-to-walling it in the streets a month ago for Mardi Gras. That was no doubt the reason their area had been hit so hard in the past few weeks.

"Break it up," she called out to the group.

"No gatherings allowed. You know that," Ben Turner added in a loud voice as he took several steps ahead of her.

Several women in the group turned their heads to look at them and Lia's heart stopped. Their eyes were straight outta *Supernatural.* Red, glowing and freaky as fuck. The energy surrounding the gathering was dark and malicious.

Two of the four guys present jumped into action and ran straight for them. Training and instinct made Lia jump to the left and dart behind a parked car. She pulled her Smith and Wesson and poked her head around the bumper.

The two men reached Turner and tackled him to the ground. Muffled popping sounds had her pulling back. She had no idea if it was Ben or one of the other guys shooting a weapon, but she wasn't going to take that chance.

"Shit," she cursed under her breath. Another look told her Turner was the one that discharged his firearm. If the guy gasping for breath off to the side of him was anything to go by.

The remaining man had Ben's arm in his grip and was bending it backwards. Natalia took aim, but before she managed to pull the trigger a loud snap followed by a crack echoed through the area.

Ben kicked the guy and Lia lost her shot of the fucker attacking her partner. Ducking back behind the car, she pressed the radio on her shoulder and called in a 10-999 to get an ambulance to Ben right away.

The sounds of fists hitting flesh told her they were still fighting. Getting to her feet, she held her gun in front of her chest with straight arms. A boot slammed into her hands before she managed to take a step in her partner's direction.

One of the women must have heard her call in for help and had come to take care of her. Lia lost her grip on her weapon and it went flying out of her gloved hands. Breathing heavily, she turned with the momentum of her body and ducked as she spun.

Catching the woman off guard, she kicked out her foot and swiped the lady off her high-heeled boots. Unease raced up her spine when the perp landed on her back and she didn't make a sound as her skull played bouncy ball with the cement.

The woman jumped to her feet and snarled at Lia. She charged toward her and tucked her hand behind her back. Good thing she'd grown up fighting her two brothers. Lia was prepared for the sharp and shiny the perp pulled out a second later.

Not that her brothers threatened her with knives. But

they always had something behind her back to torment her with, so she grew up jumping out of the way before anything really registered.

The first time they'd pulled this trick with her she stood there staring and got a face full of super worms they fed to their bearded dragons. The second time she was covered in slime. The third time she'd jumped out of the way.

Jumping onto the hood of the car, Lia was in a perfect position to kick the woman in the head. The perp's hand completed its swing. Two things happened at the same time. The sound of metal scraping metal was loud in the night and Natalia's foot hit a cheek resulting in a loud snap.

The woman's head flew to the side and she fell to the ground. Lia jumped from the hood and landed on the woman's head but couldn't stop to wonder how much more damage she caused. Another guy was headed toward her with a loud shout.

Lia ran away from the gathering and down Royal street. The man chased after her. The yank on her shoulder turned her into a ballerina pirouetting as if her life depended on it.

Left to her knight stick, she yanked it from the loop on her belt and swung as she twirled. A fist connected with her face with enough force to make her see stars.

Before the stars in her vision stopped twinkling warm bands wrapped around her like she was a present. "Not today, Satan," Lia snarled.

"Lucifer isn't here yet. My master is summoning him as we speak," the guy replied. His rancid breath warmed the side of her face and made her gag reflex do push-ups in the back of her throat.

Swallowing the moisture pooling in her mouth, she turned her head to try and see who had her. Her eyes halted on the site of Ben lying in a pool of blood ten feet away. Her partner's fingers were twitching in her direction but based on the amount of red surrounding him she wasn't sure if he would make it.

The guy holding her grabbed hold of her mask and pulled it from her face. "Asshole," she gritted as the elastic wrapped around each of her ears to hold the white cup in place scraped her skin. It wasn't as if it hurt all that bad. And the least of her worries at the moment was the virus.

Her stomach joined in the reflexes making her gag. As they ping-ponged around and sent bile surging up her throat, Lia realized she wasn't likely going to make it out of this alive.

Refusing to give up so easily, she pretended to give up and went limp in her captor's arms. He turned with her and faced the mansion on the corner. They hadn't made it more than a few feet. She got a view of the other side of the house.

A sting on the side of her neck registered and she cried out in pain. A sickening sucking sound told her the guy holding her was drinking her blood. The warm trickle that rolled down her neck confirmed that theory. Fuck that noise.

She had been willing to wait for the right moment to break from his hold. Losing patience, she reached up and clawed at his face. Her nails scratched over his face, making him lift his mouth away from her and curse.

"You aren't to feed from the tributes," one of the other males chastised the guy holding her. "Bring her inside."

"Looks like you got lucky...well, for now," the voice growled in her ear. He shifted and took a step toward the residence. It was then that she noticed a red light glowing in one of the front windows of the LaLaurie mansion.

It consumed her attention for several seconds while she watched the four other men and remaining woman entered the open front door. A lightbulb went off in her head. It was more of a neon marquee that said: YOU GO IN THERE YOU WILL DIE.

Warm liquid trickled down her neck and under her uniform top and Kevlar vest. The flow increased as she wiggled and kicked and fought to get free. She hoped her call for help meant her fellow cops were on their way to help her.

Dread was a thick soup in the air as they crossed the threshold into the house. The guy carried her to a room on the right that felt as if the devil himself were living there.

She'd always felt a sense of malicious energy surrounding the building, but this was that times a million. Her heart stampeded against her ribcage when she saw the massive creature standing in the middle of the room.

The scent of rotting meat had her stomach churning like a washing machine on the spin cycle while pained moaning echoed around the space followed by growls and cries. The combination made her skin pebble with goose bumps while her heart raced in her chest.

When she focused in the darkened room all she could initially see was red eyes. Exactly like they men and women had. Okay. Not exactly like theirs. This beast's eyes radiated power that felt like knives against her skin and made her heart skip several beats.

The massive thing had gray skin, bright red hair and sharp black horns on its head. Her first thought was that this was the devil. And her second was that he was summoning more of his kind from Hell.

When she was carried through the arched entry and into the room, she saw more details. Whatever was happening here was going to be even more of a game changer for the world than COVID-19.

There were symbols scrawled in blood on the floor in a circle not three feet from her. No doubt they'd used the blood of the people bleeding all around the pentagram on the wood floor.

There was so much blood in the room she tasted copper

in the back of her throat. Or maybe that was just bile. Her gag reflex was working out so much it lost its extra weight around the middle.

The guy holding her dumped her on the ground. She landed in a puddle of blood. It splashed onto her face from the force of her impact and made her lose the battle with her stomach.

Turning to the side she opened her mouth and threw up the red beans she'd eaten for dinner. "We need more blood to break the spell on Lucifer. Use her," the demon barked at someone.

She wanted to get up and run but she was busy being sick. When hands grabbed her, she threw her arms up in defense. A blade slashed through her arm as it covered her neck and head. The hand holding the blade lifted and removed the knife from her flesh.

On the return she didn't move fast enough and cried out when the weapon plunged into her side. She kicked her leg out and rolled to get away. A foot stomped on her shoulder then kicked her in the skull.

Darkness dotted her vision threatening to take her under. She fought with all her might and forced herself to remain still. If she continued fighting, they would keep stabbing her.

Agony shot through her side. She had no idea how to tell if she was mortally injured but figured her best bet at this point was playing dead. When hands grabbed hold of her, she went completely limp and bit her lip to keep from crying out when her side protested.

Electricity zapped her when she was dumped on top of the symbols. The demon thing started chanting in a foreign language and wind started ripping through the room. Someone must have opened the window.

Or not, she thought as she watched the red lights turn black. The pentagram brightened and smoke drifted from the center of the circle. It was all she could do not to cough against the stench that now filled the room.

It was as if roadkill was tossed on a roaring fire. Keeping her eyes partially closed, she watched as forms shifted inside the symbols. The chanting increased along with the winds. The entire time Lia felt her blood pumping from her veins and running into the circle.

Her life's blood seemed to feed whatever the demon was doing. The electricity intensified to the point she almost crawled away from the source. Thankfully, she was able to adjust when the wind moved all of the bodies.

With a hand now clamped over her side to stem the flow, Natalia watched in horror as a massive figure rose from the smoke and lights. It was an angel. Not, she corrected he just looked like an angel.

There was nothing peaceful about the evil that flowed from his presence. Massive black wings stretched wide behind his back and a smile broke over the handsome face. She couldn't see the color of his eyes, but thought he had black hair.

"Earth is finally mine," the devil purred. "I will enjoy killing my father's favorite pets…what? No!" The roar shook the windows and made the front door slam shut. She had no idea what was happening, but the second the devil tried to step from the circle he was sucked right back inside.

A blast of malevolent energy exploded throughout the room. It was so powerful she had no doubt it traveled for miles outside the walls. The demon in the room roared and was pulled inside the circle with the devil.

The second both were gone the remaining people looked around the room bewildered. Lia swore they had no idea what to do now that their master was no longer there.

She shifted to get up. Or tried to. She'd lost too much blood and couldn't move. Her limbs felt like cinder blocks and weighed her down. The sound of sirens kick started those left behind. As they took off, Lia tried one more time to crawl to the door.

She couldn't move. Not even to press the button on the radio at her shoulder. Every small move she made caused her hand to move slightly and the flow of her blood to increase.

Suddenly it was all just too much. The black spots expanded in her vision and her heart stuttered in her chest. Her last thought before she succumbed to the darkness was that she hoped her colleagues found her so her parents could bury her. She didn't want them to worry about where she was.

CHAPTER 2

*A*raton lifted the rocks and two fingers of Lagavulin to his lips and listened to the females in the room talk about making the homecoming perfect. Why the fuck would they worry so much about making her return a happy event? The child would be ecstatic to be home with her family.

She'd lived without most of her relatives and even her parents at the end of her stay in Khoth. Something happened. That was what the whispers and tense atmosphere was all about. He had no idea what exactly happened. But knowing how important it was for her parents to keep her safe from the demons hunting her…it had to be bad.

He'd been alive more years than he cared to think about and had been a Warrior Angel most of that time. It was his job to assess scenes in an instant and analyze what didn't fit.

After all demons weren't known to be honest and straightforward. Especially the Daeva demons that looked human. Most often very attractive men. He made the mistake of trusting a good-looking woman when he was a very young Warrior. Unfortunately, he still had the scar on his side to show for it.

The sound of wind came rushing through the house from the entryway. Araton set the glass down and ran out of the kitchen and into the hall. The second he reached the large foyer he saw the blue-green-purple lights like the aurora borealis off to the side of the black double front doors.

Cailyn moved around the wings Araton hadn't realized he'd extended. Habits and all that. He'd even automatically conducted a scan for demonic energy. When nothing pinged his Spidey senses he forced the red feathered appendages away and kept watch.

"Welcome home," Cailyn greeted and hugged Isobel as they walked through the portal that was created to get the Vampire Royal family from Scotland where they crossed the portal from Khoth.

Then her mother, Elsie behind her. The child that fled to the dragon realm of Khoth for her safety a couple years ago had aged far beyond the time she'd been gone. Of course, Araton knew that was because time moved differently in Khoth as opposed to Earth.

But it was one thing to see the evidence in person. Araton didn't expect to see a young woman walk through the door. He still saw her as the precocious little girl that was filled with Godly energy and joy.

Araton cocked his head and considered what was before them. He and his brothers had come to Zeum that night as protection. No one was taking any chances with the child turned young woman that was the embodiment of the Goddess Morrigan's power.

"It's good to be back," Izzy replied, but her affect didn't fit with the words. Araton recalled the huge smile he'd seen on her face the last time he'd seen her. Her dark curly hair matched that of her father, the Vampire King who walked through the portal right behind Elsie and Izzy. The large male was holding his son as if he might be taken from his arms.

Even the baby Cian, looked older than when the couple had left. His brown hair was longer, and his clear blue eyes tracked everything around him. It was the way he scanned the room with purpose that spoke volumes. It was also the fact that he'd grown several inches.

"We made some food. Are you hungry?" Illianna, Araton's sister asked Izzy. He could tell his sister was aware of the change in the Princess.

As a Joy bringer, his sister was created to bring others happiness. Because of that she no doubt felt the extreme change in Izzy. Araton was geared for anger, rage and killing. And for the first time since he met the child, he sensed those emotions vibrating under the surface.

Whatever happened to bring her home had hardened her. Brought out rage where there previously wasn't a hint of it. He'd expected her to return from Hell a changed female, but that didn't happen.

He couldn't imagine what caused her to withdraw into herself like this when being held captive in the ninth circle of the Underworld and surrounded by Behemoth demons with massive teeth and horns had not.

Araton's palm itched for his sword of fire. He wanted to eradicate her enemies. A familiar bloodlust surged in his chest. The need to kill something was both invigorating and infuriating. He might have been born a Warrior Angel, but he wasn't born with murder in his heart.

Murderous rage enveloped his heart when his sister had been kidnapped and taken from them. Araton searched high and low and questioned countless demons in his hunt for any clue about Illianna's whereabouts.

For a century he'd believed she was dead, but he couldn't

leave it alone. His family needed to know what happened and be able to grieve. It was Rhys, a half-demon hybrid that found her in a sex club in Hell that brought her home.

Araton stalked back into the kitchen and grabbed his glass then added a couple more fingers. Sipping the liquid, he was about to return when the others made their way into the spacious kitchen.

"I made your favorite," Cailyn was telling Isobel as she carried her baby on her hip into the room. Araton again marveled that her son, Liam was born close to Cian, but Cian looked so much older. "Although, I'm sure your mom's is much better. I followed the recipe as closely as possible."

Elsie took Liam from her sister and cuddled him close. Shae came in a few minutes later with Maddox toddling beside her. The female vampire had scars on the side of her neck that she used to hide with her long red hair.

Araton recalled the stories of her kidnapping and torture by an archdemon named Kadir. One that Isobel incidentally killed with a touch. Perhaps he was wrong about her homicidal tendencies. No, he decided. She didn't harbor the darkness in her heart that was there now.

Very quickly the room was crowded, and he had inched his way to the enclosed patio off the kitchen and was watching through large windows. Isobel stood there with little inflection as those around her joked, drank and ate.

Rhys brought out his *hey juice* and offered a glass to Izzy which was followed by a chorus of "Fucking Rhys."

Araton turned away from the celebration as he tried to calm his raging need. Izzy's internal struggle was fueling his own. It was easier to scan the tile floor with the replica of the Triskele amulet that used to be the Tehrex Realm's connection to the Goddess.

So much had changed since that day he, Ayil and Abraxos confronted Rhys about being complicit in kidnapping their sister. Angels used to keep a distance from humans and paranormals alike. Now their lives were so intertwined Araton wondered what life was going to be like in ten, twenty years.

His brother Ayil was mated to a Phoenix named Kennex. His sister in law created quite the buzz in Heaven when she bombed their park. There was always something eventful happening there and he was surprised this took the cake. Shortly before Kennex smuggled her explosive device to Ayil's house in heaven, Ramiel, an Angel of Retribution, mated a Fallen Angel that had earned her wings back when she helped rescue Izzy from Hell.

Of course, it wasn't the first time his family was the center of attention, so he shouldn't have been all that surprised. They seemed to have a knack for attracting dangerous, questionable beings. His sister Illianna wasn't exempt to that either. She had mated a cambion which is a human-incubus hybrid, after Rhys was responsible for finding her when angels failed for over a century. Araton owed the male more than he could ever repay for rescuing his sister from unspeakable torture in the second circle of the Underworld.

Abraxos joined Araton in the patio. "You going to come back and join the celebration?"

"I'm checking the property line for demons. Now that she's home they will pick up on her energy signature," Araton informed his brother. It wasn't entirely a lie. He was crossing to the windows as he spoke to scan the area.

The grass, trees and lake in the distance all looked peaceful. The training center, Anthru House, was ablaze with lights and Araton noticed the kids leaving the front door followed by a male with black hair.

"Did you notice anything different about the Princess?" He asked his brother.

When Abraxos didn't respond right away, Araton turned

to see his brother checking out Izzy through the windows. He knew the look on Abraxos's face. His brother was considering something that he would lose a nut for if he followed through.

"She's a child," Araton chided as he headed back toward the kitchen.

"She might have been when she left, but she's grown up now. And, yeah. Her energy is off," Abraxos agreed. "Could be because she's grown up and smokin' hot now."

"Do not let her father or Rami hear you say that about their little girl," Araton warned. The two males had been enemies so to speak when they met. Isobel brought them together and eliminated their differences.

Ramiel used to be a human named Dalton who was married to Elsie years ago. Dalton had been killed by skirm. He was made an angel when his soul cried out at the injustice. Speak of the angel.

Ramiel landed in the back yard. His massive black wings illuminated by the lights on the corner of the mansion. His mate, Zakara landed next with her purple, diamond studded wings. Both entered through a side door a second later.

"Hey guys," Rami greeted as his wings disappeared. "I think we can relax a little. There aren't any hint of demons converging on the house. I think the spell Pema and Isis cast on her is working so far."

Araton nodded and kept his mouth shut. He wasn't going to be the one to tell Ramiel his beloved Izzy wasn't the same. The male would learn that and seek vengeance which was what his kind excelled at.

"Good to see you guys again. I brought tiny lemon cakes," Kara told Araton as she held up a pink box.

"You are a Goddess," Araton told her. "I'm so glad the archangels pulled their heads out of their asses and gave you your wings back." And he meant it for more reasons than her pastries. She was a good angel with a pure heart. She sacrificed everything to save Ramiel and Isobel.

Araton followed the new arrivals into the kitchen, so he could snag a treat. The conversation when they entered stopped. Izzy looked over and her lips lifted at the corners and tears glinted in her eyes. She was in Ramiel's arms a second later with Zakara next to them.

The relationship between the two was unlikely and a result of Rami's trial to earn his black wings. Every Angel of Retribution had to earn his position to ensure they didn't abuse the power given to them.

The door to the patio opened and several footsteps echoed across the tile. Araton acted on instinct and had his flaming sword in his hand by the time he turned around. The male with black hair that he'd seen hoofing it over from Anthru House stared at this wall-eyed with his hands in the air. He was a cambion, but Araton didn't get the same sensual vibe others of his kind threw off. Normally, their kind gave off vibes of an erotic nature and ramped up the sexual energy around them. Not the case with this one.

"I came to greet the Princess. And some of the trainees wanted to say hi," the male blurted.

Tristan stepped up behind the cambion and clapped him on the shoulder with a smile on his lips and in his blue eyes. "It's okay, Araton. You can put your weapon away. Schmidt here is the new training coordinator for the realm."

Ah. Schmidt was Nikko's replacement. It was an unwanted reminder of the loss of their friend. Sadness permeated the room for several seconds before little Brantley raced through the door and headed straight for Gerrick.

"Uncle, uncle," Brantley called out.

Gerrick laughed and picked up the kid then tossed him into the air. Araton didn't think anyone else could fit into the kitchen, but he was proven wrong when Orlando and his mate Ember walked in hand in hand.

"What's up little guy? Want a cookie? Looks like Kara brought some goodies."

"Yes, yes, yes," Brantley begged as his little hands opened and closed rapidly. His grey eyes were unique with their gold flecks. He was surprisingly happy for a kid that nearly died with in his mother's womb. It was a testament to how much Orlando and Ember loved their adopted son.

"Oh, did you bring chocolate cupcakes?" Ember added as she rubbed her slightly protruding stomach.

Kara opened the lid on the box and nodded. "I sure did. I thought chocolate killed dogs though."

Ember threw her head back and laughed. "It does. Shifters, however, can eat anything they want. And this little one loves chocolate. And sweet and sour soup."

"You're pregnant?" Izzy asked with a smile. It was a relief for him to see the excitement from the Princess. He was worried about her but had to hope she would be okay with time.

Orlando walked over and hugged Izzy then grabbed a cupcake for his mate and a cookie for Brantley. "Yes, we are. She's due in three months."

"Congratulations," Isobel replied then turned to Schmidt. "And, welcome to the family. In case it wasn't obvious I'm the Princess, Isobel. I've recently returned home from…Khoth, the dragon realm." There was no missing the despondency in her tone of voice when she spoke.

It had Araton itching to kill whoever caused the sadness for the Princess. Shaking his head, he grabbed a lemon cupcake and peeled the wrapper away and took a big bite.

"God these are delicious," he said at the same time Ember groaned in delight. They both chuckled and looked at each other.

"I think I am going to have to try one," Izzy said as she reached in and picked up a pink one. "Are there any signs of demons?" She asked Ramiel as she removed the wrapper on her treat.

"No. I didn't pick up any signs," he replied.

"I don't sense anything either," Araton added. "The lake looks clear, as well. Your energy is…different. I wonder if it will ping them in the same manner as before."

Isobel cocked her head and licked frosting from her upper lip. "What do you mean different?"

Zander stepped forward and laid his free hand on Izzy's shoulder. "I'm sure it's nothing, *nighean*."

"I'm not the same as when I went to Khoth. And, before when Troy…right before we left Khoth I couldn't feel the Goddess. What if I no longer carry her energy. What if he killed it?" Tears brimmed in her eyes and she set the half-eaten cupcake down on the counter.

"No, sweetheart," Elsie interjected. She was no longer holding baby Liam and she wrapped her arms around Izzy. "You are the same beautiful Izzy as always. You've grown into a strong, intelligent female. Nothing will ever change that. I know for a fact that the Goddess would not forsake you for what happened."

The last words were whispered into Izzy's ear, but every supernatural present heard the words. It was confirmation that something had indeed happened in Khoth. It broke his heart and made him angry that such pure joy had been tarnished.

"You're right," Izzy said and pulled away from her mother. After wiping her eyes, she picked up the cupcake and continued eating. He could tell it was difficult for her, but she was trying to erase the tension from the room. It was a testament to her strength that she refocused the conversation and got the party rolling again.

If Araton ever discovered who had harmed Isobel he would rip the fucker to shreds. Her father and Guardian angel would have to get in line behind him. They'd tainted a pure soul with shadows it never should have possessed and that was not something he would ever forget.

CHAPTER 3

"Fucking demons," Abraxos grumbled. "There was a fiery Phoenix waiting for me in San Diego and I had to cancel because they can't take a break for one damn day."

Ayil turned and smirked at their brother. "It's better this way. You couldn't handle the burn."

"Like Hell I can't. You aren't the only one equipped to pleasure a Phoenix. I was born for everything female," Abraxos countered. It was always the same thing with his brother.

Ayil never fed into Abraxos's addiction to females until he found his mate. And, he wanted that for him, but his patience for the sappy only went so far. They were bred to fight demons. It was their mission to strike them down and protect humans and supernaturals from the vile creatures.

"This is not the time for this shit. According to Gabriel he suspects there was a breach of the veil closing off the Under-world," Araton barked getting them back on track. Or trying to.

Abraxos shook his head. "Brother, you need to get laid.

The tension you are rocking is making my skin itch. I'd say we can find you a woman to fuck, but there aren't many humans out right now. And the supes are steering clear of the streets, as well."

Araton's molars ground together to keep from snapping his brother's head off. He couldn't recall the last time he'd had sex. It had been decades, maybe longer. Who the hell had time for that when demons were infiltrating the planet in droves?

Besides, he was never going to lose sight of what was important. Bad shit happened and innocents paid the price when he got caught up in anything other than his mission.

Don't think about that right now. If he went too far down that path he would be sidetracked. Not something he could allow when they were heading into an unknown situation.

As they flew above the metropolitan area, Araton recalled the last time he'd seen the streets so empty in the Crescent City. There was a time briefly after a Hurricane a couple decades ago, but that was entirely different. The last time the streets had this same feel to them had been during the time of the plague.

Everywhere they went on Earth streets and parks were bare. Restaurants and bars were closed except for picking up orders. Very few places had their doors open at the moment. Droves of humans were contracting a virus and becoming ill. Medical systems were overwhelmed, and people were dying as a result.

Bourbon street was just below them and was completely empty of revelers. Demonic energy was faint, but distinct below them. He knew the house they were headed to but landed in the middle of the road near Marie Leveau's House of Voodoo.

His brothers landed beside him and glanced around. "Why did you land here?" Abraxos asked.

"I sense demons, but it isn't strong enough to say whether or not it's just skirm. Do you detect something more?" Ayil asked.

Araton extended his awareness and didn't have to work as hard to sift through the crush of bodies that usually roamed the French Quarter. It made his job far easier. Off to the left he picked up on the presence of supernaturals. Likely gathering at Old Absinthe House.

It was Abraxos's favorite bar, aside from the old blacksmith's shop turned bar. He needed to keep his brother walking or they would end up dragging him from the place. An energy signature to their right had Araton in action before he really thought about what he was doing.

The dark alley between two buildings was the perfect hiding place for the skirm he saw crouched in a doorway. Gotcha, motherfucker. Araton had his flaming sword in hand, but before he could take the minion out, Aison jumped into the fray and plunged an enchanted titanium blade into the skirm's chest.

The minion flashed on fire and was ash in the blink of an eye. The blade wasn't the strongest weapon the Dark Warriors could have used, but it was the only one that caused a chemical reaction in skirm that made fire blaze through them in an instant turning them to ash. Made cleanup a fucking breeze.

Slate was behind Aison with his hands in the air. "Shit, sorry. Didn't see you guys there."

"That's because we were hidden from sight," Araton replied as he stowed his angelic weapon.

"What brings you to our fair city?" Aison asked as he twirled the *sgian dubh* in his hand.

"There was a major surge in demonic energy suggesting an archdemon breached the veil," Ayil explained as they all headed out of the alley.

"That's what we sensed," Slate said as he looked at his fellow warrior. Slate's hazel eyes scanned their surroundings as he walked while Aison did the same.

The warriors were highly vigilant, reminding Araton why they'd ingrained themselves in the alliance. Angels weren't officially on team DWA, but he and his brothers worked closely with the group.

Not only because their sister was mated to a Dark Warrior in Seattle, but because they fought the very same entities as he and his brothers. Araton appreciated their zeal for killing demons. It matched his own.

"What do you know?" Aison asked. Araton slid a gaze his way, taking in the powerful wolf shifter. His closely cropped black hair matched his animal's fur. Araton had seen him shifted once before and marveled that his dark brown gaze lightened when he shifted.

"The disturbance occurred at the LaLaurie Mansion and was one of the strongest Gabriel registered in a long time," Abraxos informed them, suddenly all business. The encounter with the skirm refocusing his brother from sensual pursuits to the business at hand.

"Why is it always that place?" Slate interjected with a shake of his head. "That house is like a magnet for evil."

"There's no like about it," Araton replied as he hooked a right and headed down Governor Nicholls. The quiet was eerie. And heavy. It went beyond simple silence. "The location was bathed in blood from the moment it was completed. We might have destroyed the archdemon influencing the previous owners, but their deeds left a stain on the place."

"As if patrols couldn't get any harder right now. More and more skirm are taking risks of exposure and breaking into homes to feed. I am really damn tired of wiping memories." Slate growled. "Did Gabriel say if Lucifer was able to break through to this side?"

Allowing his gaze to scan the area, he continued to search for malevolent energy. As it always did in this city, there was malignant energy in the air. It likely had to do with the ghosts, demons and supernaturals that congregated there. It was the perfect place if you asked him.

Aside from having unique architecture that he loved, everything there had vibrant energy in the wood, steel and concrete that surrounded them. The energy was a mix of light and dark that oddly enough soothed his restless soul. Likely because he had always been surrounded by both.

The gas lamps on the homes flickered in the cool evening air as they walked. Araton loved New Orleans. The Spanish style homes, and Cajun food were unlike anything found anywhere else in the world.

About a block and a half away he paused along with his brothers and the Dark Warriors. "We're going in to clear the house first. You guys make sure there are no lower level demons or skirm hanging around," Araton instructed Aison and Slate.

Slate ran a hand through his brown hair and shifted his head around the area. After several seconds he sighed and nodded. "We will give you fifteen minutes then we are coming in. And, don't forget about the attic. That's usually where they conduct ceremonies."

"The humans do. I doubt the demons will need to be that close to the epicenter of evil," Aison countered.

Araton opened his mouth to argue but Ayil clapped his hand on his shoulder, stopping the words. "I will personally check the attic while these two scour the rest of the house."

Araton headed across the street and didn't bother hiding his presence as they stepped out from the shadows. It took too much energy and there was no one around. He nearly fell on his ass the second he stood on the side of Madame LaLaurie's mansion.

The demonic energy was suffocating. He stumbled and fought his gag reflex bouncing in the back of his throat. In all the centuries he'd been fighting demons there had never been a signature this strong.

"Fucking hell," Abraxos ground out as he braced himself against one of the windows of the house. He hissed and lifted his hand a second later. "I hate to say this but Gabriel might be wrong about Lucifer."

"No, he's not wrong. The Rowan sisters also cast a spell binding him to Hell. Between that and God's force keeping him in the Underworld it's not possible that he escaped," Ayil added.

"There's only one way to find out," Abraxos announced and hurried around the corner. His skin crawled and his stomach rebelled against the evil as he opened the door.

It felt as if he walked through a gelatinous barrier made of acid when he stepped over the threshold. Agony washed through his wings making his heart race. It was a good fucking thing he'd had centuries of ignoring pain to continue his fight against demons.

The scent of sulfur and smoke increasing sent off an alert in his brain that had him rolling before he even knew what he was doing. His wings didn't retract so the blood on the floor smeared across the feathers. Given the pain lancing his right wing he guessed some of the blood was demonic.

His sword of light was out and slicing through a hellhound before Araton managed to get a full view of the room. He was on his feet and kicking the two halves of the demon dog aside. He didn't have the time at the moment to plunge his flaming word through the creature's heart to disintegrate the fucker.

His weapon was designed to kill creatures from the Underworld with ridiculous ease and would eliminate the need for cleanup when they hit the heart or head. Sounds echoed behind him and he knew by the light energy that it was his brothers entering the house. At the same time, his sixth sense told him there were other enemies nearby.

Araton continued through the dining room and into another room. He had no idea what it was used for normally, but it had been converted into a demonic temple. There was a large pentagram along with symbols drawn in blood on the wood floor.

The sound of one of his brother's heading up the stairs was hardly noticeable from his position. Wherever the demon was hiding it was doing a phenomenal job of remaining silent. Lower level demons were incapable of stealth.

Turning another corner, Araton's heart clenched at the proof that they were too late. Easily a dozen slaughtered humans were scattered around the floor. Throats sliced open. Skulls cracked with brain matter all over the floor. And Stomachs were gaping with entrails spilled on the wood.

A creak behind him had him swiveling as he leveled his weapon at his enemy. Matted black hair flew around wide green eyes. The human female fell on her ass barely missing the cut that would render her to ash.

Araton lost his balance as he pulled his arm back to avoid harming the innocent. His mind stowed the blade before he was even aware of giving the command. His wings flared wide to help him catch his balance.

The female cried out as she landed and fell to her side. One side of her face was black and blue while blood poured from a gaping wound on her side. Something in Araton broke at the sight of her barely hanging onto life.

He'd taken a step toward her and was stopped when claws raked across one of his wings. "Fuck," he roared and called his weapon to his hand.

The screech of the demon was loud in his ear. As was the

sound of demon flesh sizzling. Thanks to the proximity of his flaming sword he was treated to eau-de-barbeque. Of the rotten meat variety.

And, cue the bile gymnastics again. Araton flipped the sword in his palm and thrust the blade behind him. His feet were in the air and he was moving before the demon hit the ground.

When he landed, his eyes found the source of the disturbance. It was a Daeva demon. The stunning female had a beautiful exterior over a rancid core. Black blood poured from a wound in its shoulder.

"Did Lucifer cross over?" Araton demanded.

Araton sent his senses out not wanting to be taken unaware again. He didn't pick up on anything on his level. Yelling echoed from the upper floors, making Araton want to rush to his brother's sides. He could kill this Daeva and head up to help, but that would mean leaving the beautiful human female unprotected. And, every part of him objected to that possibility.

"Fuck you, angel. I don't have to tell you shit," the demon spat then screamed when he stabbed through one of her thighs. He hated her kind of all demons. They hid their evil nature beneath a beautiful exterior. Countless humans had been lured in by these monsters. No doubt most of the humans lying dead on the floor had been brought here by this vile creature before him.

"You want to try again? We know you cast a spell to open a portal for him. What I want to know is if it succeeded," Araton demanded.

The Daeva smiled up at him while arching her back. The move exposed more of her cleavage. As if he was distracted by an attractive female. He never had been and never would be. *Liar.*

He recoiled at the silent admonishment. He glanced over

his shoulder to the human female and noticed she was watching with wide eyes.

"The devil didn't make it," she whispered.

Turning back to the demon, Araton smiled. "Guess I don't need you after all." His flaming steel pierced her heart and a scream echoed before she burst into flames and disintegrated.

Rushing to the human's side, he crouched next to her and ripped his shirt from his back and pressed it to her side. She hissed and groaned. "You're safe now. That demon that lured you here is gone and never coming back. Can you tell me what happened here?"

"That bitch didn't lure me here," the human choked out. Sweat beaded on her brow to mix with the blood and grime smeared all over her body. Araton had the absurd urge to pick her up and comfort her. "I'm a cop. Officer Natalia Olsen. I came to investigate. They killed my partner."

Araton stiffened when a sob left her, and tears brimmed in her eyes. Had he pressed too hard? He lifted the corner of his shirt and was surprised to see the bleeding had slowed.

Abraxos and Ayil came running into the room a second later and stopped short when they saw him. Abraxos shook himself and continued to their side. "I've got her," his brother told him.

Araton looked at his brother for a minute and pressed the cloth against her flesh once again. "Which one is your partner, Natalia?"

"He's not in here. He is out on the street with the people I had to shoot." She closed her eyes and laid her head back.

"There are no bodies out there," Abraxos informed her. "How's your head? Looks like you took a hard hit to the face."

"Like I have a house sitting on my face. Backup must have cleaned the scene up. Shit. I need to report into my chief," Natalia blurted and tried to sit up.

Abraxos caught her arm before she fell back to the ground. He and his brother eased her to a sitting position and Araton lifted his shirt again and noticed she had stopped bleeding.

Tossing the cloth aside, he wondered how he managed that. He wasn't a healer. He should have offered her no comfort from the pain she suffered, yet he couldn't deny that she was breathing easier.

"You can't tell your chief about any of this," he told her.

"I have to. They're all in danger. As an angel, you should be all about protecting us humans, right?"

Araton glanced over his shoulder and wanted to curse his lack of forethought. "I am a warrior angel as are my brothers. Our job is to kill demons. Now, you said the devil didn't cross over. What happened?"

Shaking her head, Natalia lifted her shirt and looked at her side that was now nothing but a scab right under the edge of a thick black under shirt. "How did you do that?"

Abraxos ran a hand down her arm. "Angel blood. My brother was bleeding, and some was on his shirt when he pressed it to your wound. Can you tell us what happened?"

She looked at Araton for several seconds then told them how they'd arrived on scene to find several people that sounded like the archdemon's skirm. After a brief encounter broke out, she was drug into the house where she was stabbed and added to the pile. What sounded like a Behemoth demon tried to summon Lucifer and when the spell failed, he was sucked back to hell with Lucifer.

"I have to call this in," Natalia insisted.

Araton shook his head. "That isn't going to happen and before you start yelling, this is for their safety. We will handle the scene. Can you get Slate in here? I want him to erase her memories," Araton asked Ayil.

Natalia jumped to her feet and swayed for a second

before she thrust her hands on her hips and scowled at him. "You aren't taking a fucking thing from me."

"Trust me. You don't want to have these memories," Araton insisted.

"You don't get to decide that for me. I refuse to have any memories erased. I'm no danger to you or anyone else. Demons are another thing altogether. It's my job to protect the citizens of this city. I can't do that if you take these memories from me," Natalia argued.

Slate, Ayil and Aison came to a halt in the doorway a second later. "She's right," Abraxos countered. "She survived a demon attack. Besides, I doubt they will be able to erase anything after you gave her your blood. We're immune to magic, remember?"

"Dammit," Araton cursed. "Fine. Let's burn this shit down and we can go back to Les Augres and see about the rest. We cannot stand here any longer and argue about this."

Araton had no idea what effects his blood would have on the human. Did that change her biology? He could ask Jace. The male would know, or at least be able to runs some tests.

"You aren't burning this house down. You can't. I can call in a cleaning crew," the human female countered.

"Your crew can't cleanse the demonic energy infused in this place. Demons will continue to use this place for evil purposes. And, my flames will erase this place from existence."

"You won't be able to burn it down," Aison interjected. Araton shot a glance at the Dark Warrior. "We've tried every kind of flame possible, but nothing has worked. There is something more at work here."

"We will see about that. Let's get out of here," Abraxos said as he started for the front door.

Natalia stared at Araton. "Surely you don't want this paragon of evil in your city any longer."

"No. I don't," she grumbled and followed his brothers and the warriors outside. Araton used his flaming sword and lit the bodies on fire and headed out the door. Fire raged inside as they stood on the opposite corner and watched.

A voice echoed from Natalia's shoulder. "It's my radio. Fire department is on their way." Sirens sounded somewhere in the distance, but before any trucks arrived the fire died out.

"Told you," Slate added. "Let's go. I have some questions for the human cop."

"I can't leave," she complained. "I have to let them know I'm alive. I can catch up with you guys. Cause I have questions of my own."

The cop was right. He didn't want her boss or family to worry. If they had discovered her partner dead earlier, they were likely searching for her right now. "You guys go on ahead. I will wait with Natalia and bring her to the house."

Sirens blared in the night air and Araton forced his wings away with a wince. The claw marks hadn't healed yet and it hurt like a bitch to put them away. His brothers grabbed hold of the Dark Warriors and turned them all invisible before they headed to the Dark Warrior Alliance's New Orleans headquarters.

The night had taken a sharp left and for Araton what remained was a case of what-the-fucks. The demons had come close to bringing Lucifer to earth. Dozens of humans were dead, and he couldn't take his eyes away from the human cop.

Her black hair was matted with blood. There was a black and blue lump on the side of her face, and she wore a wicked scowl. He wasn't the one fascinated by females. So why couldn't he look away from the beautiful human?

CHAPTER 4

*A*s he got closer to Bienville and Bourbon Dante contemplated continuing to Royal street to join Slate, Aison and Illianna's brothers. From the reports something big was going down. Unfortunately, his need for sex clawed at his body, pushing him close to the edge. He needed sex soon or he was going to be a danger to everyone around him.

That was the downside of being what he was. He loved being the Cambion Lord most days. Since losing one of his closest friends he wanted to be anything but the leader of his kind. As an incubus-human hybrid, sex was Wheaties to his kind. But he'd lost interest after Nikko's death.

It was a Goddess damned tragedy for him. A female's body had always been his Nirvana. Yet duty had become his mistress of late. Not that he hadn't been driven by a desire to make a better life for supernaturals in the realm.

Ever since he'd escaped the Underworld after his mother sent him to live with his father, Dante had been determined to improve life for cambions. Zander helped him create his position as Cambion Lord to provide structure where there had previously been none.

When he came into his power as a young man he was overwhelmed by his inner demon. Unaware he was anything more than a human boy, he ignored the cravings for sex. Initially he believed he was possessed by the devil. His mom treated him as if his head turned in a circle. It was unacceptable to have sexual relations with anyone outside marriage and when he coaxed several women into his bed, his mom sent him away.

At the time he had no idea how she reached out to his father. Later he discovered incubi bred with humans as a permanent portal for them to cross over to earth. They were one of the few demons that often crossed thanks to that biological connection. It was why most incubi readily responded when their offspring were in distress. They took the opportunity to mold their children in their image.

Dante knew right away he had no desire to be like his father. Taking what he needed without compunction was not who he was or who he wanted to be. There was nothing that could justify rape in his mind.

Just call him a pioneer. The first thing he did when he escaped his father and returned to the realm was to establish a friendship with Zander and Nikko. It was at Zander's prompting that he decided to create a refuge for cambions.

Nikko actually came up with his title of Cambion Lord saying all leaders needed a label to signify their station. He was living in Nikko's barn when the archdemons attacked and killed all the leaders at that time. Most of his closest friends were elevated to positions of power and together they created the Dark Warrior Alliance.

Life changed for him pretty quick after that, and he never looked back. He'd worked hard to create a safe place for cambion stripling to go when their transition hit. He spent most of his time looking for humans who transitioned into sex crazed beasts thanks to their demonic parent.

Now things were different. His life was no longer about sex. When Nikko had been killed, he stepped up and took over half of his duties for the alliance. He wasn't cut out for training new recruits, so he left that to Schmidt. He was the most focused cambion he had. But wicked smart and patient enough to deal with overeager striplings.

Dante only handled the strategic side of assignments and finding new recruits. Making sure the Dark Warriors in each area had what they needed and moving them around when necessary. How the hell Nikko did that and recruited new warriors was the eighth wonder of the world.

It was utterly impossible in Dante's opinion, yet Nikko had handled it like a pro. He missed his friend more than he ever imagined possible. It seemed as if he was picking up his phone to ask Nikko for advice every time he turned around, only to put it down when he remembered he was dead.

With a sigh, he pulled the door to the bar only to find it locked. Stepping back into the street, he checked the sign to make sure he was in the right place. Yep. Old Absinthe House. What the fuck was going on?

Glancing around he checked the empty streets. Dread had him stopping as his heart skipped several beats. This city was never this quiet. Had the demons managed to kill all the humans in the quarter?

His skin prickled like it did when skirm were nearby, but it wasn't as if the numbers would explain the absence of life around him. As he opened his senses and searched for any signs of life, he realized several things at once.

First, he forgot about the shelter-in-place order the human governments had instituted to deal with a virus that was spreading rapidly through their population. And second, there were supernaturals in the lower levels of the club engaging in sex. He could feel faint traces of the energy. Just being close to sensual acts fed him small amounts of energy.

Finally, the upper level demons were no longer in the area. During his time in the Underworld he'd honed his senses where malevolent creatures were concerned. It was the only way to escape the worst abuse in Hell.

Like all good cambions, Dante had his inner demon trapped within a cage in his mind and it now battered against the cage the walls. He sought a way in the building through the inner courtyard. The bar was established over two hundred years earlier by two cambions he discovered and took in. Because of him Pedro and Francisco avoided quality time in the second circle of Hell with their succubus mothers.

Because of their need to feed from various creatures, the two opened the human bar on the top floor and the supernatural one below ground. Dante had been there countless times over the centuries but had to admit he preferred Confetti Too to this place.

Everything in the French Quarter was clustered together. Normally, it made his stomach twist and his heart race. Because of the eccentric nature of visitors to the city most supernaturals were able to hide in plain sight. That should ease his discomfort, but it didn't. Unlike Hayden, the shifter Omega; Dante didn't agree with coming out to humans. They were too volatile and explosive.

Once inside the hidden oasis between buildings, Dante had to smile at the groups standing around chatting with drinks. Pedro and Francisco were losing half of their business daily, but they found a way to make up for that. Shifters, Phoenixes, imps, and Valkyrie talked and drank various beverages while sitting at wrought iron tables set up throughout the enclosed garden.

There was no sign of the various enchantments these

beings would normally employ to avoid detection. Part of Dante was ready to shed the tension and dive into a night of pleasure, but the rest of him couldn't let go of the vigilance he'd wrapped around himself when Nikko died.

"Dante," a Valkyrie called out and waved her hand.

Turning his head, he forced a smile across his face. "Paige? How are you doing?"

The Valkyrie smiled and leaned forward on the table. The movement pushed her breasts out and put them on display. Perhaps this wasn't going to be a waste trip. Her arousal and desire hit Dante with a punch of energy. It lifted his mood and cleared his foggy mind just enough for his smile to become genuine.

"Better now that you're here. It's been what? Two decades?" Paige asked.

He nodded recalling the last time he ran into her in New York city. They'd spent a wild weekend together. "About that. Last time was when we saw Rent. Or tried to. I don't think we left the room for three days."

Paige laughed and nodded her head then talked about the crème brulee from room service. As she talked her wings fluttered at her back. The opalescent appendages reminded him of dragon fly wings. The first time he met one of her kind he'd wondered how such small wings held them aloft and allowed them to fly around. He quickly learned they were as formidable as the female warriors.

"I need to go see Pedro and Francisco, but I will be back soon. We can catch up," Dante promised.

Nodding, Paige got to her feet and ran her hands over his shoulder. "I look forward to reconnecting. You look like you could use a boost, and I'm more than happy to provide it," Paige purred with a sensual smile. Dante leaned over and kissed her briefly, enjoying the boost of energy.

"I'll be back before you know it," he promised then headed into the building.

Standing at the door, Dante looked down the back hall. In the distance he caught sight of the wood bar which proudly displayed its centuries of use. The antique fixtures were off, but with his keen eyesight he could see the jerseys and helmets hanging from the exposed cypress beams of the ceiling. The familiarity brought comfort he needed as he struggled with who he was and what his purpose was now.

It was a chore for him to set aside his maudlin thoughts and continue onto the janitor's closet. Twisting the handle, he hoped Clarence was still watching the entrance for the club. He'd been there from the beginning of the place. It just wouldn't be the same without the tiny male.

Pushing the panel open, the smile widened on Dante's face. "Clarence, my friend. It has been too fucking long. I see you guys have made some changes," Dante observed. Before the brownie could respond a shifter female opened the door carrying a tray full of drinks.

The four-foot male rushed past Dante and opened the outer door for the waitress as she walked outside. He clapped his hand on the male's shoulder as he passed back toward the inner door.

Clarence smiled wide, revealing his yellowed, blunt teeth. "It's good to see you too, mate. I'm doing well. With the human world in a veritable stand still, Pedro and Francisco expanded their supernatural section. I would ask what brings you here, but I can see from your aura that you need to feed."

The elf-like creatures had the ability to see people's aura and work earth magic so it was no surprise that he could see how bad off Dante really was. Not that he needed to hide what was happening, but for some reason he didn't want anyone to know how much he was struggling lately.

Shrugging his shoulders, Dante flashed one of his smiles.

It never failed to attract males and females alike. Not that he wanted the small male, but he wanted to put him at ease. "It seems there are fewer unmated females in the realm since the mating curse was lifted. Please tell me this is still the place to find the hottest females in the city."

Large brown eyes narrowed as he smiled. "Of course, Pedro and Francisco attract the best looking in the realm."

"And are your bosses here? I need to ask them about demonic activity in the area."

The brownie nodded his bald head. "They're at the usual table in the back.

"Thank you," Dante said as Clarence muttered words in his native tongue. Within seconds a door appeared where there was once a smooth wall. The smell of sex, sweat, cigarette smoke, and alcohol hit him the moment Clarence opened the glowing door.

A steep, stone staircase led the way to the revelry below. Torches hung on the walls, providing the only illumination. Dante hurried down becoming more and more invigorated as he went.

The bump and grind of bodies enveloped him as he reached the bottom step. It was shocking to see so many together in one place after seeing the empty streets and businesses above. The supernatural floor of the club was much like upstairs, with the antique wood floors and large bar area. It was missing the sports paraphernalia because the clientele down here had vastly different interests.

Sure, they enjoyed human movies, music and sports. But that was one minor part of their lives. Supes were directed by their natures. Like cambions needing sex. Valkyrie thrived on combat and battles. Shifters had to feed their animalistic side while vampires drank blood.

Supernaturals came in all shapes, sizes, and colors. Most of them couldn't blend in with human society without drawing attention, so they rarely had contact with the human world outside of television.

The atmosphere of the club was intimate which only served to highlight what he'd been struggling with. He blamed his identity crisis on the fact that he was surrounded by mated couples. It was another reason he had taken the job of supervising the various compounds.

He crossed the busy dance floor and he slid into the booth across from two of his favorite people in the realm. "Dante." Pedro boomed with a smile.

"We didn't know you were in town. When did you get in?" Francisco asked.

"I arrived day before yesterday. Checking how shit is running in your area," he replied with a shrug of his shoulders.

"Should we have this conversation after you feed?" Pedro countered. "You're on the edge of losing your shit."

Dante laughed while inside he was cursing himself. He should have known they would sense how close he was to losing it. He'd taken them in and taught them everything he knew. "Nah. Paige is waiting outside for me. I like your expansion, by the way."

A female fire demon approached the table with an apron around her waist. Fire demons had flawless, luminescent skin and earthly beauty that masked their deadly interior. Only idiots pissed one off. Or masochists. Dante knew quite a few who enjoyed pain during sex, but few enjoyed regenerating burned flesh. Rhett showed him how loyal they were. He was really fucking grateful to have the lethal but fun male on their side.

"What's your poison, darlin'?" the fire demon asked as she cocked a hip, bumping Dante's shoulder.

"Whiskey, please." Dante said then refocused on his friends when the waitress walked off.

"We've wanted to do tables outside for our main customers, but with humans all over the city like fleas on cats it was never safe. It's more than made up for not having the top half open right now," Pedro explained.

"Has everything slowed in the city? And, by that I mean has there been an increase or decrease in demonic activity," Dante clarified as he thanked the waitress for his drink.

Francisco was nodding his head while Pedro was smiling at a female sitting at the next table. "I haven't run across a skirm kill for a couple weeks. At first, I assumed it was because there weren't as many humans out and about at the moment. But that's not it," Francisco told him.

Refocusing on the conversation, Pedro added, "Tonight was the first time in days I sensed skirm nearby. I've only encountered half a dozen hellhounds and rage demons in the past couple days when normally I hear about at least one per day. This city is a hotspot for activity, as you know."

"Yep. It's where all the legend and lore comes from," Dante acknowledged. "So, why do you think there has been less activity lately? Supernaturals, which include those vile fucking creatures, are immune to the virus affecting humans." This was why he'd come here. He wanted their opinion. They'd been in the French Quarter for centuries and had seen countless wars and plagues.

Witches, warlocks and sorcerers all across the globe had been casting spells to seal portals that let demons in from the Underworld. The problem is no one really knew if they were working or not. It had never been tried before. Not until the Rowan sisters were successful at binding Lucifer to Hell.

"Honestly, I have no idea. I'd say your warriors have been too efficient at killing the enemy for the past century, but it doesn't feel like that's all of it," Pedro said as he ran his finger around the rim of his empty glass.

"I think it's the new archdemon. Ever since she lost her

sister, she has been focusing solely on Seattle and kidnapping stripling," Francisco interjected.

"Lower level demons follow orders from the top, so that makes sense," Dante murmured as he tossed back the rest of his drink. That actually did make sense. "If you hear anything about this please give me a call."

Dante excused himself and headed back to Paige. He couldn't put off feeding any longer. With Izzy back in the realm it was more important than ever that he understand what motivated their behaviors. No one was willing to put the Princess at risk. Not only was she their tie to the Goddess, but she was loved by everyone who came in contact with her.

CHAPTER 5

What the hell happened? Was she in a coma and this all a dream? Or worse. Was she dead? One of those had to be the explanation. Nothing else made sense for what she had seen tonight. She wasn't surprised by any of it. She'd grown up on stories of the fantastic.

But being introduced to these sexy men and angels was somehow surreal. The three brothers were obviously other, but she had no idea about the other two men. Slate and Aison. Two others joined them, Luke and Micah. All seven guys were dressed in leather pants and black shirts with thick soled boots.

"How are you not freaking out?" Araton asked a moment later as if the angel could read her mind. He'd introduced himself along with his brothers and the Dark Warriors with them.

They were sitting in the parlor of a mansion in the Garden District. She'd driven by this house countless times on patrol. Never before would she have believed that super-naturals lived in the place. It was elegant with furniture she'd only ever seen on TV shows about rich people's houses. The odd thing was she didn't feel unwelcome or uneasy in the place.

"I was born and bred here in the Crescent City. I was raised on ghosts, vampires, voodoo and Cajun food. And in my line of work I've seen my share of ghosts and vampires. Seeing angels is actually comforting," she admitted as she waved to the sexy, broody angel.

There were three of them with red wings that filled the room, making it seem small in comparison. She was in a freaking mansion with a formal parlor bigger than her entire apartment, yet their presence took up all the space. And that was without adding the others. She had no idea what they were, but her gut screamed they weren't human.

"You've seen vampires?" Slate demanded.

She shrugged. "As a cop I've one or two guys with pointy teeth embedded in a woman's neck. I assumed they were fake, but he looked up with red eyes and took off faster than I could keep up. That told me all I needed to know."

"That wasn't a vampire. It was a skirm. An archdemon's minion," Araton informed her.

That made sense. Her skin had crawled when she encountered these creatures. The women had been whisked away to deal with their injuries and when she read the Detective's reports later, she discovered the victims reported being attacked by what they called vampires.

"So, demons live on earth? Did they all come through the LaLaurie Mansion? Cause that would make sense about why it's haunted and evil follows it like a plague. I'm just glad that Lucifer never made it through. I watched his ass get sucked back down to Hell along with the other creature," she said and couldn't help the shudder that ran through her when she remembered the ugly beast with horns.

"There are many more portals from the Underworld, but most often they occur in a place infused with foul energy.

And only a place of pure evil would be dark enough to allow Lucifer to cross over," Araton explained. "Which is why I wanted to burn the fucking place to the ground."

Lia crossed her arms over her chest and narrowed her eyes at the angel. "I understand your desire, but someone owns that home. It's not right to destroy something that doesn't belong to you. In my opinion that would perpetuate the evil aura around the place."

Abraxos, Araton's brother, chuckled at that. "I like you, Natalia. You have spunk. You're not just another beautiful face. And, you have a point. There are many other ways to cleanse a dwelling, but they take time and a lot of power. If I agree to remove as much of the malicious energy as I can, perhaps you'd be willing to help me refill my stores."

Natalia thought she heard a growl from Araton but couldn't be sure. What she did know was men were the same regardless of their species. There was no doubt what Abraxos meant. His smoldering smile and hooded eyes told it all.

She lifted the corners of her mouth. "Sure. If you promise not to destroy the house."

Araton definitely growled then, but Abraxos swaggered closer to her. "I promise to minimize damage to the structure while clearing dark remnants. Tell me. Do you like candle-light dinners?"

"Nah. Too much fuss. Besides it's not me that will need a meal after. I make a mean red beans and rice. Let me know where to drop it off and you will have your sustenance," she countered.

Ayil and Araton both laughed at that while Slate and Aison joined in. Abraxos's expression displayed his surprise before it softened, and he was smiling at her again. Before he could respond the sounds of the door opening had everyone looking to the arched entry. A couple seconds later another good-looking man walked in and stopped short as he smiled at them.

"Hey there. I didn't know you guys were in town. Good to see you all again. And, who's this stunning beauty?"

Natalia felt erotic heat fill the air like steam and she felt her body responding despite her attempt to squash the desire. Never in her life had she reacted so strongly, and she wasn't that attracted to the new guy.

Araton was the one who'd grabbed her attention from the second she laid her eyes on him. Her core had clenched, and her stomach fluttered even as she had wondered if he was another demon. Wings and good looks didn't mean shit as she'd discovered when the other woman showed up at the house.

"This is Natalia Olsen. Lia. This is Dante Tresan, the Cambion Lord of the Tehrex Realm. This lovely female is a New Orleans Police officer and a human female," Araton interjected. "She survived two archdemons as they tried to summon Lucifer from the Underworld." Was that pride she detected in the angel's voice?

"Wow. You must be one tough female, Lia. When was this? I see the bruises on your face and blood there on your clothes," Dante gestured to the slice below her bullet proof vest. "Zander should have warned me. I would have gone there first."

"He isn't aware of what went down. I haven't had time to update him yet. We just got here," Aison replied.

Dante's head shot back to her and zoned in on her side where the knife shredded her insides. "How are you not bleeding all over the leather sofa?"

"I inadvertently gave her my blood," Araton replied with a pinched expression.

"Which is why I can't erase her memories," Slate added.

"What are you? How can you erase my memories?" Lia blurted.

"I'm an actual vampire. We drink blood, but only that of our kind. And we never kill when we feed. We also can't turn you into a vampire. You have to be born that way. Garlic doesn't affect us. Neither do crosses. But the sun thing will char us and turn us to ashes," Slate told her with a smile as he leaned against the fireplace mantle.

Her mind was rapidly reaching its capacity. There was a throbbing in her injured cheek and it only added to the ache inside her skull. "I'm not surprised Hollywood has it wrong. I have so many questions which I will get to later, but first I want to know what a cambion is and what the rest of you are. I take it you aren't human like me. No way does a normal guy look like you all."

"A cambion is a half-breed," Araton explained.

"We are a breed of incubus or succubus and human," Dante cut in with a glare at Araton. "We're the lovers of the supernatural world. And, before you ask. The Tehrex Realm is what we call the collective of species here. Basic ally, the supe society on our planet. There are other realms that exist on other planets," Dante said with a dismissive wave of his hand.

"So, you're like a sex demon?" She clarified, ignoring the comment about other planets. That was too fucking much right now.

"Cambions aren't demons. We have souls, and most prefer not to harm others to get the energy we need to survive. An incubus or succubus would not hesitate to rape whoever they needed to survive. I'd rather die than do something so despicable," Dante spat in response.

Araton moved a few steps so he was between her and Dante. She made a note that the Cambion Lord was testy when it came to the topic of demons. She sensed deep rooted issues around the subject. There was no way for her to begin to understand where they stemmed from.

The sight of a rusted blue Nissan Sentra distracted her and made her jaw clench. If a guy with shaggy blonde hair was driving it, she was going to run. Or shoot the driver. She had to tell herself not to grab her gun and pop the tires. That was thanks to an ex-boyfriend. When her fists clenched in her lap and her head throbbed even more, she shook herself. That was in the past.

"I'll come back to the other planet things another time when my mind is able to comprehend the idea. Tell me about these demons and why they're fucking with my city," she demanded.

"Shit has gone sideways in the Underworld over the last few years," Dante began.

"Lucifer has been freed from his frozen prison in Lake Cocytus ever since the Vampire Princess was rescued from the ninth circle of Hell," Araton said as he interrupted. The angel kept looking at her and moving closer. He'd take a step to her then two away. She had no idea what to make of it. "The Rowan sisters managed to send a spell with the angel that saved her, and it bound the devil to the Underworld."

"Having freedom to roam every circle of his realm wasn't enough for him," Ayil added. "He wants to cross over to Earth so he can claim the planet and all of its inhabitants."

"He wants to make his father's favorite creation pay for making him love them more," Araton finished.

"I take it we are God's favorite creation," Lia replied having followed what they were saying. "But, isn't God your dad too?"

The three angels shook their heads. "No. We aren't original creations. We have parents who were," Araton explained.

"Well, we can't allow Lucifer to make it here, so how can I help?"

All of the guys in the room glanced at one another and it was Araton that shook his head and replied to her. "No offense, but there isn't much you can do to help us. We have it handled."

"I don't think you do," Lia informed them. "You had no idea the demons were killing humans tonight. And, none of you arrived in time to stop anyone from being killed. I was there. I fought their skirm, or whatever and survived being attacked."

Araton clenched his jaw and narrowed his eyes. "We aren't omniscient, but neither are you. You got lucky tonight."

Slate stood up straight and held up his hand. "We have been trained to fight demons and their minions. Our Goddess tasked us with protecting innocents. Human and supernatural alike."

"So, you all know about the deaths in the cemeteries? Because I guarantee they have something to do with this bullshit," Natalia couldn't help but point out. She hadn't put the pieces together until these guys started talking.

"What do you mean? Cemeteries are hallowed ground. It would do the demons no good," Araton pointed out.

Lia stood up and pointed at the angel's chest. "And, what would happen if dozens of people are killed in one?"

Araton looked at his brothers who had their eyebrows lifted to their hairline then he turned back to her. "It would shift the focus to something foul and dark they could use for their malevolent work. If the demons were able to claim the grounds, they could then use every soul buried there to give them more power…"

"And a pure soul stolen for evil purposes carries more power when their family gives them over freely. When someone is murdered, they instinctively hold onto their lives with everything they have," Ayil cut in.

Every one of the guys in the room had gone pale. Lia lifted a hand to her mouth as her gag reflex was hard at work once again. Her heart started racing and sweat broke out over her brow. "How easy is this to do? Cause there have been eight murders in Cemetery number one in the last three months."

"I have no idea. It's never actually been done. Each time a funeral occurs the land is blessed anew and that provides protection. Plus, demons have to sacrifice themselves in the process. Not many are willing to do that." Araton explained.

"You said Lucifer is now roaming all around Hell. Maybe it's harder to say no when you know he will hunt your ass down and make you pay for disobeying," Lia countered. "Regardless. You need me. I am not walking away when I know how much danger surrounds us."

"She has a point," Dante said as he walked over to a bar that was set in one corner. "Drink?"

Lia nodded right away. "Tequila if you have it, please."

"Whiskey," Araton called out, making Lia quirk a brow at him. "Just because I'm an angel doesn't mean I hate alcohol."

"I have so much to learn," Natalia muttered under her breath.

"Yes, you do," Araton replied as he stared at her. "You can be a part of this, but you will be working closely with me. I won't have your blood on my hands."

"Are you sure about that, brother?" Abraxos asked while Ayil was eyeing Araton in a way she couldn't decipher. She was going to do what she could to kill demons with or without them. It would be impossible for her to walk away and never look back.

"We can't have her running around on her own. Without removing her memories, she will just get into trouble," Araton reasoned.

"Can you read my mind?" She blurted when he voiced the very thing she'd just been contemplating.

"Vampires can read minds, but angels can't," Slate replied as he smirked at her. Yeah, he'd been listening to her plans.

She shrugged and turned away. "He's right. I can't just forget this shit. Mythological creatures are real, and demons are killing in my city. It's my job to protect the citizens."

Araton mumbled something under his breath that she couldn't catch and kept his gaze trained on her. "You will do everything I say when I say it. Got it?"

"Yes sir. I'm not stupid. I need you to train and guide me," she replied as her mind went over what the fuck, she had just gotten herself into. "Now that that's settled, I need to call my chief. He has to be worried about me."

CHAPTER 6

$\mathcal{A}$raton watched Natalia as she exited the human hospital. Her black hair was hanging over her shoulders, but out of the tie it had been in previously. For a second he thought she cleaned herself up until he noticed the locks were still matted with blood and dirt.

His heart did something he hadn't experienced since the first time he faced a demon many millennia ago. It skipped several beats. He found he didn't like the dark circles under her green eyes. And, his rage rose when he noticed the bruises still on her face.

The realization that none of that detracted from her beauty in the least had him scowling and itching to stab something. He didn't do romance like Abraxos, yet he couldn't deny wondering what he would need to do to get this human cop into his bed.

A male embracing her had him holding his breath to keep from acting out. Of course, a woman as sexy as she was would have a mate. Or a spouse as the humans called their partners.

It was when they parted, and she waved then turned

toward Araton that he realized her shirt was different. She was no longer wearing the black button up shirt of her uniform. The grey t-shirt made her look softer than before, but there was no denying the steel in her spine as she headed to their rendezvous spot.

"Araton," she whisper-yelled as she reached the corner of the parking lot.

Araton let go of the spell hiding his body but kept it on his wings. "I'm here. What did the doctors say? I still think you need to return home and get some sleep."

Shaking her head, she unlocked her car. It was a patrol car for her position as a police officer. Popping the trunk, she tossed the plastic bag from her hand into the dark space.

"The doctors said I have a concussion which means I shouldn't go home and sleep. Besides, I can't sleep yet. My chief just told me there were other sites of ritual sacrifice in the quarter. We need to check them out," Lia insisted as she slammed the metal and headed to the front of the car.

"You are still in no shape to face demons again so soon. How many sites were discovered? And, what did they look like? This might be a crime committed by your kind and not demons," Araton pointed out. He needed to get the information and then he would leave her here while he cleared the scene. He refused to place her in anymore danger.

"There were four spread throughout the French Quarter, but the biggest was in Jackson Square where all the vendors usually sit and sell their wares and the fortune tellers read your palm or do tarot readings. There was another at St. Louis Cemetery number one and another on Bourbon and Canal," Lia told him.

Araton nodded and reached out to his brothers. They appeared next to him a second later. Lia gasped then growled, "Warn a girl would ya? You almost gave me a heart attack."

"There's no time to walk you through every step of this process. If you insist on being part of this investigation you need to expect the unexpected," Araton told her with a biting edge to his words. It pissed him off that he considered taking time away from their task of finding and eliminating the demons to tell her more about how shit worked in their world.

He nearly asked Abraxos or Ayil to take over working with Lia. He hated how soft he was becoming. There was no time for anything other than killing the vile creatures of the Underworld.

When he ignored his duty, others paid for his mistakes. The reminder was seared into his brain forever. He needed to keep remembering why he never strayed from his mission. That was the best way to keep Natalia safe.

"We're sorry," Abraxos purred and stepped closer to Lia. When his brother brushed dirty hair away from her face, Araton smacked his brother's arm.

"There are at least three other locations that are sites of probable demonic rituals. I'm heading to Jackson Square. Ayil, you go to the first cemetery. And, you search Bourbon and Canal, Abraxos," Araton instructed.

"I told Dante and the others to make another round on the streets," Abraxos added. Let's meet up at your place at the end of the night."

"Good idea. I'm going to be sticking around until we are called somewhere else," Araton told them.

"I bet you are," Abraxos said while he waggled his eyebrows.

"Asshole," Araton growled and punched his brother in the face. He'd taken off before Brax could retaliate.

Lia's voice was loud below him as he shrouded himself in invisibility. "What the fuck just happened? Wait. You can't go without me."

Araton's keen hearing allowed him to hear Abraxos's reply as if he were still standing next to them rather than flying away. "That was my brother being the moody asshole he's always been. You can head to Jackson Square. He'll meet you there. And, by the way we cleared the malevolent energy from that house as much as possible. I'm not sure it did much. We're going to check again in a few hours after things have a chance to settle into the new norm for the place. But the house is standing like you asked."

Araton shut them out and opened his senses as he flew. When his demonic sensor pinged in his head, he slowed and circled a row of houses near where the levee broke during Hurricane Katrina.

Landing in a backyard, Araton remained hidden and followed his nose to the stench of brimstone. He didn't need to use his extra senses to find the house he needed. Hovering outside a back window, he saw at least eight skirm gathered in the living room.

Opening the back door, he dropped the spell and had his flaming sword in his hand. He slashed through the first minion to approach him. The second threw a blade that Araton dodged. Well, he thought he did.

When it hit his right wing instead of missing him, he growled and kicked into high gear. Arm swinging faster than the skirm's eyes could follow Araton cut through the minions with ease. His heavenly weapon acted like a titanium weapon, in that it turned them to ash.

Within seconds he had killed every last skirm in the house and went in search of their master. Kicking the pile of dust as he walked through the kitchen, he tried to detect any demonic presence in the home.

In the living room there was a pentagram on the floor and blood splattered on the walls. It smelled like old blood, telling him it was from at least a few days ago. A quick search of the lower level revealed two dead bodies, but nothing else.

Upstairs there were clothes and blankets scattered throughout each room except the master bedroom. There he found a large bed with dark bedding. The smell of blood was strong here, as well. There was a darker stain on the comforter told. When he touched it he noticed how stiff it was. Given the odor permeating the room he figured it was likely blood.

When he encountered nothing else in the home, he was outside and in the air in a heartbeat. The night was quiet for this area. He stayed at his home close to Les Augres Manor several days a month.

His favorite residence was the one he had in Heaven, but this was his second favorite place to visit. It was the energy of the city that called to him. One thing he never got when he was here was silence. In the Garden District there were often tourists walking through the area.

At night he was used to flying over the French Quarter which boasted music, dancing, laughing and drinking all hours of the night. Seeing humans live so vibrantly was another reminder about why he stayed true to his calling.

Landing in the middle of Jackson Square he wasn't surprised to see Lia already there. She swiveled around and gaped at him. "I thought you'd already be here. I can see why you took so long to get here," she muttered as she reached up and plucked the knife from his wing.

"Fuck," he cursed as pain blasted through his side.

"The scene isn't as gruesome as the last one," she informed him getting right to work. "There are puddles of blood and a large pentagram, but no bodies."

Araton followed the direction she was pointing in and first noticed the yellow police tape then saw the rest. The blood gleamed in the moonlight. He expected to smell death permeating the area like in the house, but all he smelled was Hell. Rotten eggs and sulfur. Made his stomach turn while tensing his muscles.

"That doesn't fit the rituals. There are always bodies. Did your colleagues take them away?"

Lia shook her head as she leaned down and looked at the pentagram. "They would have, but my chief said they were out searching for the people that were killed here. Murders in this location are not a common occurrence. Why here? Sure, wars and deaths occurred here, but it's not like some other places in the Quarter."

"Demons always have their reasons. Although, they don't make sense most of the time. The bigger rituals, like bringing Lucifer to this side, will be done in locations aligned with evil. What the fuck?" He blurted and knelt next to her to get a better look at the symbols.

"Who else were they bringing over from the depths? I've never seen archdemons brought over so publicly," Araton growled as he stood up and scanned the area.

Taking a deep breath to calm himself down, he realized supernaturals had been here. He made a mental note to remind Dante and Zander to inform their citizens the need to report immediately when they see shit like this. They might have been able to stop the demons if they got here fast enough.

"What are you talking about?" Lia asked. He hadn't realized how close they were to each other. Her sweet scent replaced the rancid ones and made his cock twitch in his pants.

Jumping to his feet, he took a couple steps away. There was no time for sex. Demons were roaming the city. "The demons rarely open a portal for their brethren to cross over in such an open location. They don't want to be interrupted."

"Well, it doesn't sound like they're very smart. Maybe

they assumed it was safe with so few people out and about right now. Can you tell if their spell was interrupted or not? We need to find them if new demons crossed over."

For the first time since meeting her, he agreed whole-heartedly. "They're definitely here. The lack of bodies is still a mystery, but the energy of this site is still so high I'm shocked the pentagram isn't lit up anymore. In fact," Araton replied then held up his hands before throwing Heavenly energy at the spot.

Natalia shrieked and jumped back while patting her head. "Asshole," she grumbled as she watched closely while the white energy consumed the blood and cleared the stench.

"Is this a normal night for you? Cause this shit is unreal." Lia walked around the entire circle of his energy and stopped halfway back to his side with eyes like wide saucers. "Crap. Someone's coming. You need to make that go away. Now," she commanded him.

It wasn't often that he was given orders like that. Especially not from a female. He was certain he half fell in love with her at that second before he pushed those feelings aside and glanced over his shoulder.

"I've already used my power to shield us from view," he assured her. The people heading their way moved with grace and efficiency telling him they were supernaturals. "But, don't worry they're like Dante and the Dark Warriors."

She squinted as she looked at the group of seven crossing near one of his favorite restaurants. Okay it was more of a café with about four items on the menu. But he could live on beignets, so he considered them a food group.

"How can you tell they aren't hu…like me?"

Araton stepped closer to her and allowed her scent to surround him. It wasn't so bad explaining things to her after all. And, with this knowledge she would be able to protect herself from danger in the future.

Pointing over her shoulder he said, "See the way their steps are smooth? Supernaturals have an innate refinement to their moves. And they move faster than humans, as well. If you look close enough you can see how their eyes have a subtle glow."

"Got it. So, they're the good guys," she remarked as her shoulders slumped ever so slightly. "I didn't find any clues that would help us identify who did this. Which makes sense now. Humans always leave clues behind. How do you start an investigation like this?"

"We tease out scents so we can identify who is responsible. But, honestly, we follow demonic signatures. For us we never find a fingerprint or smoking gun that points the way. It's all about the…fucking hell," he cursed when he caught the scent on the breeze. "Get out of here. And, call Dante," he blurted and tossed his cell phone to Natalia. She caught it and immediately hit the contact.

But she didn't move. She stood next to him which made him reluctant to leave her side. The way the supernatural heads lifted into the air told him they smelled them nearby. Dousing the rest of his Heavenly energy, he released the concealment spell on them and had his flaming sword in his hand.

"Dante. Araton said you need to get to Jackson Square. I think there's something wrong with some of your people or whatever," Lia told the Cambion Lord. Somehow, he wasn't surprised she understood without him telling her more.

The second he got a clearer picture of those coming for them he realized they were possessed by upper level demons. He'd never heard of that happening before. A vamp bared its fangs and sprang into the air.

Araton lifted ten feet into the air and took off toward the vamp. With ease, he sliced his head from his shoulders. A scream from Lia iced the blood in his veins and made him turn sharply. The move pulled a muscle in his wing which forced him to land.

He was thrusting his weapon at a half-shifted female that looked like a creepy mix of a panther and human. With her superior reflexes she ducked and kicked out a leg that clipped one of his ankles.

A gunshot brought his head up and he watched as Natalia held a pistol in her outstretched hands and kept pulling the trigger. The creature approaching her paused and jerked as each slug hit its chest.

One more swing and the possessed shifter was crumpling to the ground. Without pausing, Araton headed right for Natalia. He had to protect her. At her side, they stood back to back and battled the possessed as they lunged at them.

If Araton could move freely he would take care of them in no time, but he could not risk Lia. Clicking reached his ears and he wasn't surprised when the female cursed and tossed her gun to the cement. "I'm out. You have a weapon I can use?"

"You can't handle an angelic sword of fire," he informed her. "Stay close to me." In rapid movements, he jumped forward and swung his weapon and sliced a vamp across the chest then before he could think he was leaping over Lia and landing in front of her to lop the head off another supernatural.

The pheromones of a sex demon filtered through the air and he turned to find an incubus trying to seduce Natalia. Araton pulled her behind him and held her in place. Steps sounded all around them. There were still four and he couldn't be in enough places at once.

"You can stop that anytime. I'm not stupid enough to walk over to you, asshole," Natalia called out over his shoulder, making him laugh.

"I don't know how you are resisting an incubus's thrall," he called out.

"What can I say it's a gift," she said as she threw something. When the sound of a rock echoed, he realized she must have picked it up.

"You're sexy, too," Dante called out as he rushed from the alley next to the church behind them. Aison and Slate were with him and Araton was able to focus on the incubus.

"This is new. You guys get bored in Hell?"

The incubus took a step toward him, but his movements were no longer smooth and graceful. "We're close to freeing Lucifer. Our new plan will work perfectly," the incubus boasted.

"You failed. That's why he isn't here with you now. I'd remind you how futile your attempts are, but that would be a waste of breath," Araton growled with the wonderful sound of battle raging around them.

His next swing made the creature cry out when it couldn't move out of the way fast enough. With jerky moves, he came at Araton again. Did this incubus possess a cambion that needed to feed? He expected more from the being.

With ridiculous ease, Araton plunged his flaming sword into its chest and smiled at the scream that echoed through the night. Turning he watched as the rest were quickly dispatched.

"Please tell me this isn't going to be the new norm," Dante blurted. "How did this happen?"

"I have no idea," Araton replied. "I destroyed the symbols before looking for any differences in the spell used. I didn't anticipate this."

"How did the demons manage to possess and control such strong beings?" Aison interrupted.

"I don't think they were able to keep control. At the end mine wasn't as smooth as when they walked up. I think

Lucifer is trying everything he can to break through. You need to issue warnings to your citizens to remain on guard," Araton advised.

"I will call Zander right away," Dante replied. "You need to get her home. She's going to fall over."

Araton looked away from the cambion and watched as Lia swayed on her feet. "I'm fine. I want to be part of this meeting. You can't leave me out."

"I can and will. You're not fine. You need rest. You're not an immortal. How you have survived the night I have no idea, but you aren't dying on my watch. Let's go," he told her.

Grumbling, Lia said, "You will wait to have this meeting until I get some rest. Then I will be back at that house in the Garden District whether this jackoff agrees or not." The steel in her spine was fucking amazing. It reminded him a bit of Mack. After meeting that formidable female, Araton should have known better than to underestimate her.

With that she marched to her car while he followed behind. He'd make sure she got home safely then meet up with his brothers. They all needed to research what this could possibly mean before they got back together later.

He was not going to keep watch over Natalia throughout the day no matter how much he wanted to. This woman was getting under his skin and his attempts to keep her out weren't working very well. The knowledge that he would see her later made it easier to part ways when she reached her house.

CHAPTER 7

*L*ia parked the car and looked over at the stately manor. Despite needing the sleep, she hadn't been able to rest over the past few hours. Instead, she had spent the time looking up vampires, demons and angels on the internet. It was impossible to know if anything she discovered was true about the supernaturals she was once again about to face.

Anticipation had her jumping from the car and heading to the front of the white house. The wrought iron gate was low and so familiar it was easy to forget she was going to see creatures that shouldn't exist. The columns and balcony above the porch were elegant, and a sight she'd seen during her nightly patrols for years. And, not once had she suspected that what lived inside was anything other than affluent people.

The hinge on the gate screeched as she opened it. Her heart hammered in her chest as she walked up the short path. The second she stepped onto the porch Araton suddenly appeared next to her, making her scream.

The front door was yanked open and Dante stood there

with a scowl on his face. "Oh. It's just you guys. I thought demons were breaking even more rules."

"No. The human isn't accustomed to our world and shouldn't be here," the sexy angel barked while keeping his stunning gray eyes trained on her. A breeze ruffled his blond hair like a lover's caress.

One corner of her mouth lifted at the errant thought. So what if the sun highlighted his unearthly good looks. It didn't mean she should fawn all over him and lose her senses. There were honest to God demons roaming the earth intent on killing people. She couldn't ignore that.

"You're lucky I didn't shoot you. Anyone would startle when someone appears out of nowhere," she countered and strode into the house.

Araton's footsteps echoed behind her. She was surprised to see Slate and Aison at the end of the hall waving to her. "I won the bet," Dante called out behind her.

Turning around she caught the cambion's eye and had to admire how good looking he was. Especially when he smiled. Too bad she was attracted to grumpy angels. Dante no doubt had some mad skills being half of a sex demon.

"We took bets on when you would arrive. I said you'd be here before breakfast," Dante informed her as he shut the door and headed to the others.

"I'm surprised it took you this long," Araton murmured from beside her.

"I had to do some research," she admitted.

"And did you find anything?" Aison asked.

"There's all sorts of information on the internet, but I doubt any of it is accurate," she replied and stopped just outside the room. Unlike the formal parlor this room was kitted out like a command center. Most notable was that there were no windows.

When she'd passed the parlor earlier, she'd noticed there

was some kind of metal shield in place. At first, she wondered why they'd want to keep the sun out and then she recalled that the sun would turn vampires to ash.

"Natalia. Good to see you again. You look much better than the last time I saw you," Micah said with a wave from where he sat at a computer.

"It's amazing what a shower will do for you. Have you guys discovered if there are other demons in town?"

"There are always demons in town. What I want to know is where you're keeping the fucker you caught earlier," Araton blurted as he walked to the big conference table and grabbed a beignet. A cloud of white bloomed in front of his face when he took a bite and landed on the front of his shirt.

A laugh escaped her before she could stop it. "It's good to know even angels can't avoid the wrath of the beignet," she said when he lifted an eyebrow at her.

Shrugging his shoulders, Araton took another bite. "I'd have squeezed lemons on them to avoid the mess, but there weren't any available. No matter. I will never turn down one of these."

"Lemon on a beignet? That's blasphemy," she teased him and grabbed one for herself. Standing with her feet shoulder width apart, she leaned forward and took a bite. As a born and bred she knew better than to get the powdered sugar on her clothes.

"It's fucking tasty. I promise you it is nearly as good as it is without," Araton replied around a mouthful of sugared dough.

Needing to look away from the way the angel looked at her, Lia turned back to Dante who now had a cup of coffee in his hand. "As Araton pointed out we found another demon possessed supernatural before returning home last night. He's being held in a room in the basement."

"You have a basement?" she blurted. Not that it really

mattered in the scheme of things, but it wasn't common. New Orleans was built on swamp land which made basements a tricky thing being below water level.

"Magically reinforced to keep the water out," Aison informed her matter-of-factly.

"You guys will be good friends to have around," she observed. "Okay, so do we need to bring this Zander in on the conversation or can you tell me what you learned and what the plan is to deal with this."

Dante nodded to Aison who typed into the computer. A large screen slid down from the ceiling and a second later several people appeared on the screen. At the front of the group was a guy with shoulder length black hair and Sapphire blue eyes. There was a young woman next to him with curly brown hair and clear blue eyes and one next to her that was obviously a combination of the two.

"Zander, this is Natalia Olsen. She's the human cop we told you about earlier," Dante introduced.

"Och. 'Tis good to meet you, Natalia. This is my mate, Elsie and our daughter, Izzy. My *brathairs*, Kyran and Bhric, have joined us along with several others. Evzen here is the Guild Master for the Sorcerers and Hayden the Omega for the shifters. I won't bother with introducing those not on screen. It's better to get to business," Zander said in a Scottish accent.

"We have one second to acknowledge how hard this is. It is a major shock for a human to discover supernaturals exist," Elsie added. "This world isn't an easy one to learn about. Feel free to call me anytime you have questions." Lia was immediately at ease with the woman. She had an open personality which she appreciated.

"Discovering vampires and demons exist isn't all that surprising but getting used to it isn't easy. I have a thousand questions about stuff and will ask them eventually. Zander is right. We need to focus on what to do about these fucking demons threatening my city," Natalia replied.

A feminine laugh out of screen made her smile. "Now that's my kind of woman," a woman with short spiky black hair and a sleeve of tattoos poked her head next to one of the brothers. "I'll be there soon to help you kill those demons."

"I wasna aware we were heading down there, Firecracker," the brother murmured as he looked at the woman. His hard expression softened telling Lia how much he adored this woman.

"Like I'd miss a chance to kill some more of these motherfuckers. And, Harlow has never seen NOLA. I'm Mack by the way."

Lia nodded. "It's good to meet you, Mack. New Orleans is the best city on the planet. Harlow will love it."

Araton leaned forward and jumped in the conversation. "Harlow is their baby and a dragon shifter from another planet. Were you able to get information from the possessed vampire?" The angel asked and shifted the conversation to the man that seemed like he was their leader while she stood there gaping at him. Dragon shifter? Wicked cool.

Zander crossed his arms over his chest and was tapping his bicep with the fingers on one of his hands. "I was able to compel him to talk, but it wasna the demon talking. Rather it was the vampire. He told us the demons forced their way inside their bodies and that they've been fighting the possession ever since, but havena been able to do much because they are stealing most of their power. The vampire said there was a plan for a house in the quarter."

"I bet it's the site we went to last night. Perhaps they already tried and failed. Ayil and Abraxos did what they could last night to eliminate the evil energy and are back there now. They weren't certain they managed to get rid of it," Araton added.

"I think there will be another attempt there. From what Lia said Lucifer seemed as if he was crossing over before being sucked back to Hell. I think that progress excited them and are now going to try again," Dante interjected.

"We can't let that happen," Lia blurted. "They killed a dozen people to power their spell. And, made several more their skirm."

"They had female skirm," Araton said, cutting her off from saying anymore.

"That's never happened before. Skirm are always males. We must be on guard. Seems like Lucifer has taught demons something new," Zander added as he ran his hand over his chin.

"I have already checked the Mystik Grimoire and found nothing. Although there is a passage that talked about using supernatural energy for Dark spells. I'm guessing that's what they are doing, or planning on doing," Evzen explained. She had no idea what he was talking about. A grimoire was a book, so she'd say they had something that held their information.

Natalia noticed Araton pull his cell phone from his back pocket. Turning she watched as he read the screen. She wasn't surprised when he interrupted the conversation a second later.

"The house shows no signs of having been cleansed with angelic power. I need to head over there and help my brothers."

It became obvious which of the men were the top dogs in this group. They all shared a look. The slender male that talked about the grimoire looked at the much larger guy with brown hair. His eyes reminded her of a panther. Odd, but stunning. Their gaze shifted to Zander then Dante.

Zander was the one that spoke up. "I know I don't have to tell you that we can't allow the demons access to the home again. Suvi is fairly certain their spell will hold, but all magic can be broken eventually."

"That's the last fucking thing we need," Araton cursed and headed out of the room.

Lia glanced around then lifted her hand. "I'm going to make sure he doesn't destroy the place. I have no doubt I will talk to you all again." As she raced down the hall after the angel, she thought about how crazy her life had become.

* * *

ARATON LANDED in the middle of the street, noticing there were more humans out and about during the day than there had been the night before. He left his body wrapped in invisibility and headed to the front door. He walked through the door and stopped short at the sight of Natalia standing there with Abraxos.

"What the fuck are you doing here?"

Hands on her hips, she narrowed her eyes. "Same thing as you. Helping."

Araton took several steps toward her so they were standing toe to toe. Her breath was a sweet heat against his skin. "And what do you think you are going to do? You're human and have no power against demonic entities."

"I might not have a sword that burns them, but I can cut a bitch and slow them down enough for you to take them out. Besides the more positive energy in a place the better," she asserted.

He watched her for several tense seconds then nodded his head. Turning to his brothers, he saw Ramiel and Gloria were with Ayil in the main parlor where the sacrifices had been made.

"What are they doing?" Lia's melodic voice drew his gaze

back to her. Unable to resist touching her, Araton grabbed her arm and lead her to the room.

"They are drawing the evil energy from the earth and house. Ramiel is an Angel of Retribution and Izzy's Guardian Angel and Gloria is an Earth Angel. Together with Ayil they will be able to infuse Light power throughout the area," he explained.

Araton joined Abraxos, leaving Lia at the entrance. Removing the dagger, he had stuck in one of his boots, Araton sliced his finger and bent to draw Angelic runes on the floor where the pentagram had once been.

The best way to remove the Dark stain from the house would be persistent cleansing of the air through blood and magic. Same way it was tainted. His body recoiled when he first touched the floor.

Gritting his teeth, he fought the worms crawling through his veins. His movements slowed and bile rose like the tide in his throat. When his mouth filled with saliva, he had to take a break to catch his breath.

A hand on his shoulder made him look up. Lia stood there with a glass of water. "Thank you," he croaked and took a gulp then coughed as the liquid burned its way down his throat.

"Looked like you could use a pick me up," she said with a smile.

"That did the trick," he told her as he noticed the tide of bile wasn't pressing quite so strongly against the back of his throat. Taking another drink, this time a smaller one, he set the glass aside and went back to work.

Murmurs filled the room, and he concentrated on pushing Light out of his pores and into the structure of the house. He met resistance and closed his eyes, putting more force into his push.

A scream startled him from his task. He jumped to his

feet with his eyes open at the same time the other angels moved. For several seconds Araton couldn't believe what he was seeing.

Shock wore off and he jumped toward Lia. Shadows were peeling from the walls and rushing into her chest. She'd grabbed the dagger he dropped and was swinging it, but it did her no good.

Every time dark energy entered her, she screamed and jerked. Araton wrapped his wings around her and did something he hadn't done for longer than he could recall. He prayed to God asking for Him to protect Natalia. It wasn't that God didn't listen to him. He was busy fighting demons and rarely had a reason to ask for His help.

She stiffened in his hold and he grabbed her tighter then looked at his brothers. "What do I do?" The shadows continued to pour into Natalia's body. Every flinch drove a knife through his heart. He stood there helpless in every way that mattered at that moment.

Ramiel and Gloria slapped blood palm prints on the walls where the shadows escaped from. It slowed them before making them stop. Araton knelt and lowered Lia to the ground. She'd gone lax in his arms.

He brushed her hair from her forehead, noting how the locks were once again tangled. He was relieved to see no blood when he scanned her from head to toe. Her eyes were closed but they seemed to have sunken into their sockets. Her skin was pale, and her pulse was slower than Araton liked.

"Is she going to wake possessed?" Ayil asked.

"There's no demon inside her," Araton insisted. "But she is full of evil energy. And we will do whatever it takes to remove any Dark magic from her system."

Abraxos and Ramiel shared a look. "She might be beyond our help," Ramiel said as he watched Natalia.

"She isn't beyond help. She has a warrior's soul. She will fight being taken over, but we need to help her. Question is where do we get that help?"

"We're in New Orleans. There's always Marie Leveau," Ramiel suggested.

"That's an option, but I think we need to consult Camael first," Ayil replied.

"We will take her back to Les Augres for the Dark Warriors to watch over while we seek an audience with Camael then," Araton said then bent and picked Lia up. He held her close as he walked out the front door.

The world seemed far darker without her vibrant energy filling it. From the moment he met her last night she brightened everything around her. Including him. She inspired thoughts and feelings he had given up on long ago when the world was young. This beautiful female had to be okay. He wouldn't accept anything less.

CHAPTER 8

Izzy hugged her mom as she waited for fear to keep her at Zeum. Even in Khoth she stayed close to the castle most of the time. And then that fateful day happened that ruined her life. Shaking her head, she pushed aside the negative thoughts. This was about more than trying to escape nightmares that refused to let her go.

"We're ready for you guys to cross over," Gerrick announced as he held his staff in the air with Jace while they held open the Aurora Borealis colored portal.

"Zander," Dante called out and clapped dad's hand. "Izzy. It's so good to see you. Goddess I can't get over how big you have gotten."

Izzy smiled forced her body to go lax when the Cambion Lord leaned over and wrapped his arms around her body. Bile did pushups in the back of her throat while her hands itched to clench into fists. She could read the surprise of not only Dante, but also all of the Dark Warriors in the New Orleans manor. Yeah, she understood. Her parents never let her leave the safety of Zeum.

"Are you sure it's safe for you to be here?" Dante asked.

Zander ran a hand through his shoulder length black hair. "Her energy has changed. This is a test of sorts. She insisted and is as stubborn as her mother. I want to test matters when I am close to protect her."

Tears threatened and made her eyes blur for a second before she cut them off. Now was not the time to lose it. Her dad would never let her leave the house again. And, she needed to test her theory that the Goddess abandoned her.

When Troy attacked her, she tried to reach the Goddess or Ramiel and tried to use her powers, but nothing happened. Ramiel felt horrible about not being there for her when she needed him. He said he never heard her calling.

She believed him. Rami proved that he would risk his life to rescue her when he went to the Underworld and saved her. There was no way he would ignore her pleas for help when helping her wouldn't pose any risk to his safety.

Dante's laugh drew her back to the moment, and Izzy made her lips twitch. Normally, she would have laughed with him and teased her father. Keeping with who she used to be, so she avoided the odd looks and the questions, Izzy said, "It's not just mom who is stubborn. You make her look like a pushover, dad. And, Illianna's brothers already told you they can't sense the Goddess's energy like they did before. Rami confirmed that."

"She's not wrong about that, Liege," Tristan agreed from his position behind them. Her dad found Tristan during a battle on a cruise ship a while back after he witnessed demons attacking and killing people on vacation including some of his family.

Tristan used to be far older than Izzy. She recalled him teasing her and giving her piggyback rides before she left for Khoth. She returned an entirely different stripling than when she left. Now she was close in age to her friend and far more haunted than he was.

Her dad shot the young wizard a glare and wrapped an arm around her waist then kissed the top of her head. He never showed anyone except her, her mom, and her brother a softer side of himself. With everyone else he was harsh and unbending. Of course, as the Vampire King he had to be that way.

Before her time on Khoth she hadn't understood much. Not only because she'd been a small stripling then either. For as long as she could remember she felt power in her body. In fact, it fizzed and bubbled happily in her veins until Troy had attacked her.

"What's wrong with her?" Izzy blurted when the sight of a female sleeping on the couch caught her attention.

"Shadows flew into her body when the angels were trying to remove demonic energy from the house," Dante explained. "Araton brought her here for safe keeping and supervision while he went to Camael to ask for advice and next steps."

Izzy walked over to the cop and sat on the coffee table. Cocking her head, she tried to get a sense of what was going on with this woman. Kinda like her power, she'd always been able to sense evil energy. At least she thought she had been able to. She'd missed it big time with Troy.

"I don't feel anything malicious inside her. Was it demons that possessed her?" Izzy clarified.

"I got the sense that they didn't think it was a possession. That takes blood sacrifice and they were removing the dark energy from the house. Natalia insisted on being present. She reminds me a bit of Mack," Dante said with a smile. "Araton was annoyed by Lia, but secretly the angel is falling for the human."

Natalia blinked her eyes open and gasped then sat up and scooted back on the couch. "Where am I?" She asked while scanning the room. "Never mind. You're here in person.

What the hell happened? What were those shadow monsters?"

Zander walked up behind her but remained standing. "That is what we would like to know. How do you feel?" Her dad demanded. If you didn't know him and the tone of his voice you would think he was issuing orders.

"My chest and head are killing me. It feels like the one time I had pneumonia," Natalia replied and shivered then glanced around the room.

Figuring the woman was cold, Izzy looked up at Slate who was standing closest to the doorway. "Can you get her a blanket?"

"Sure thing. Can I get anyone anything else?" Slate asked.

"Some coffee," Dante requested as he took a seat in one of the armchairs in the room.

"I'll take some coffee as long as you have chicory," Lia added.

A true smile bloomed cross Izzy's face. She recalled the type of caffeinated beverage her aunt Mack brought over to Nate on Khoth. She hadn't recalled that it originated in New Orleans until that moment. She missed her friends on Khoth and her favorite haunts, as well.

"Is there any other kind?" Slate countered before chuckling and heading out the door.

Her dad ran his hand through his shoulder length black hair and sat on the love seat not far from the sofa. "It's almost nightfall. Before we head out to patrol, is there anything else you can share about what's happened in your city?"

Natalia rubbed her chest and shook her head. "Things have been off for weeks now with the virus running rampant throughout the world. Crime hasn't really gone down much despite a majority of the population staying at home. I'm inclined to take a guess that's thanks to the demons and their skirm. Until the other night I had no idea supernaturals were real. I mean I always believed they were out there, but I never had confirmation, so I wasn't searching for clues that might hint at supernatural causes. Not that I would know what to look for."

Slate returned with a blanket over one shoulder and a tray with a carafe of coffee, cups, sugar and milk. "Evil comes in many forms. It's not always as easy as saying look for the horns. Sometimes they come with a handsome smile and good looks. What I will say is you should never ignore your gut. Even if what it's saying seems like you're overreacting."

"I've seen enough in my career to know you are too right. I've never ignored any kind of warning. I knew something wasn't right at the LaLaurie Mansion, and I told my partner, but I didn't insist on waiting for back-up. Now he's dead," Natalia explained as she sat forward. "I'm going on patrol with you guys."

"Of course, you are," Dante said with a smile. "I'm going to let your angel know so he doesn't worry about you."

"He's not my angel," Lia insisted, but Izzy sensed the woman was falling for Araton as much as she suspected the Warrior Angel was for her. "Can he get calls in Heaven?"

Dante shrugged his shoulders. "No idea. I text or call when I need to and somehow, they usually show up when we need them."

Izzy's dad sat forward and leaned his elbows on his knees. "From what Illianna and her brothers said they don't get calls per se, but they hear when individuals they are connected to need them. But many angels have homes on Earth and spend a good amount of time here. Their jobs require them to be here anyway, so it makes reporting to a scene faster."

Lia sipped her coffee and they discussed areas to focus their patrols on for another half hour before it got dark. Izzy was on edge as she waited to leave the house. Les Augres wasn't as protected as Zeum and she had honestly expected the demons to make an attempt before now.

She'd been there at least an hour. The fact that they hadn't made her feel free for the first time ever as well as horrified that she was no longer a being worthy of the Goddess.

She'd always wanted to be with her friends and family without placing them at risk of an attack. Before going to Khoth she never really missed going out to the park or for ice cream. Once she had the freedom to explore more, she realized how much she missed in the Tehrex Realm.

Now, as she stood to head into the streets to patrol for the first time since returning home, Izzy wondered if she was making a mistake. She was numb inside. Unsure if she wanted to know the Goddess had left her or not. If Izzy was worthwhile, she would still have the Goddess with her.

She needed to know the risk she posed to those around her. Especially her little brother. Cian was a beautiful baby. Resolve settled in her gut like a stone. She would go on. Reclaim her life. When Donovan's grim face popped into her head, she stalked out the door ready to kill something.

* * *

Dante watched the shadows, aware Zander and Izzy were out with them. He wasn't exactly comfortable having the living embodiment of the Goddess Morrigan walking the streets with them. If the demons managed to get a hold of her, they could use her to free Lucifer.

The only reason he hadn't objected more strenuously was because Izzy had indeed felt different. From the moment she was born, he'd been drawn to her by the Light that shone from inside the little girl. Now, she wasn't so little anymore. And the Light was gone. Or muted. He couldn't really tell.

Ever since he'd seen her in person after she returned

from Khoth she was different. Yes, she'd matured and was easily eighteen years old. But, she had yet to transition. The time when stripling passed from childhood into their full powers.

Initially, he thought she had transitioned, but he realized she didn't move with the sensual grace of adult females. Or radiate sexual maturity. Not that he thought about Izzy that way, he reminded himself when his gut twisted in a knot. That was how his mind worked.

"I love the old buildings and architecture in the Quarter," Izzy said as they headed past Jackson Square and deeper into the area.

"Many of these buildings were built when I first arrived in this country. For this area that's extremely *old*," Zander told his daughter. Dante often forgot that not everyone had been around so long there were few things they thought of that way.

"Let's head to Pedro and Francisco's place," Dante suggested. He never hooked up with Paige the other day. He wasn't going to pass that up again. "They still have their finger on the pulse in this city."

"I've always wanted to go to Old Absinthe," Tristan added. "That place is as legendary as Confetti Too."

"We don't have time for you to drink and find a female to fuck," Dante warned the wizard. Even though he was planning on doing just that. Or at least he was going to make plans to meet up later.

"I hate to be the bearer of bad news, but the place is closed. It's our way of trying to flatten the curve," Lia interjected.

Dante forgot she wasn't aware of their world. Hell, she wasn't even one of them. She was a human with knowledge of the realm because her mind couldn't be wiped. Dante wondered if Araton had given her his blood on purpose.

That's an awfully big oversight on the angel's part. Dante had never known Araton to focus on anything but the fight against demons. He has a quick temper which clearly translated into a hot desire. The tension between him and Natalia was explosive.

"Och, there is a realm bar underneath the human bar. Some friends own the place," Zander explained.

When they turned down Bienville Dante was surprised to see several supernaturals not bothering to hide their obvious otherness. There was a Valkyrie with her gossamer wings on full display and a fire demon glowing in the gas lamps. Shooting a look at Zander they increased their pace to the group.

Araton appeared next to Lia as she headed across the street to a group of humans snapping photos with their phones. They were really fucking lucky the streets weren't as crowded as usual. It would be a colossal nightmare to deal with.

"Slate. Head over with Natalia and Araton and deal with those humans. Tristan, cast a spell to interrupt cell service. Can you erase the evidence?" Zander ordered the Dark Warriors.

Tristan shook his head. I can't erase what's already there. We are going to have to make them erase all traces of their images and video," Tristan explained.

"Shite. Get it done," Zander told them. Both warriors nodded and headed to the humans while they continued to the supernaturals. Dante remained on high alert. The last thing they needed was for Izzy to be abducted while they were distracted.

"What the fuck are you thinking?" Zander demanded the second they were standing next to the group.

Initially, none of them tracked what they were saying. Dante noticed the female he was looking for among them.

"You okay, Paige? What's going on?"

Zander looked at Dante, reflecting his concern back at him. Dante laid a hand on her shoulder and her head turned his direction. It was the first time she showed any sign of seeing them.

"Dante? What..." Paige murmured and allowed her voice to trail off as she stood there.

"You are all exposing yourselves to the humans. Is there a celebration we aren't aware of that makes this acceptable?" Dante asked.

Shaking her head, Paige swallowed and paled when she noticed Zander standing there. "No. We were heading to Absinthe House when we sensed...something off."

The Valkyrie next to her concealed her wings and wrapped her arms around her waist. "It reminded me of archdemons. I took off running, but don't remember anything after hitting the corner." Dante noticed the female had scars all along the sides of her neck.

His heart skipped several beats when he realized she had to be one of the survivors Zander and his Dark Warriors rescued years ago from Kadir's lair. He couldn't be certain, but he doubted many supernaturals had been attacked by demons enough to leave that amount of scarring behind.

Dante wrapped his arms around their waists and lead them to the gate for Old Absinthe. "Go in and get a drink. I can escort you home in a bit if you don't want to stay."

"Thank you," Paige told him with a small smile.

Dante leaned in and kissed her cheek at the same time he called his pheromones to the surface. He pushed them through his pores in a trickle and was relieved when the females relaxed against his side. "I was coming to see you, anyway," he admitted to Paige. "I got busy the other night. But I'm not going to let that happen again."

The fear receded from her face and the familiar scent of

feminine arousal replaced it. Dante kissed the side of her mouth and returned to Zander's side. Shit was uneasy in the Big Easy, and he wasn't sure how they were going to keep their existence hidden if this crap continued to happen.

Hayden's insistence that they come out to humans rang through Dante's head as he watched the Vampire King manipulate human memories. Was it wise to keep their existence a secret? Perhaps Hayden was right, and it was time for humans to join in the hunt.

Look at Natalia. She was a human cop and hadn't backed down from demons. Nor had she shown any fear of them. In fact, she had consistently insisted on being part of their investigations.

That didn't mean everyone would welcome their existence. Something he knew all too well. His own mother couldn't love him after discovering he was different. And, it had little to do with the fact that he had an insatiable need for sex.

She'd been horrified that he wasn't human. When she gathered the other villagers and came after him in their family home he was forced to flee to safety. It was luck that he was sent to his father. He often wondered what would have become of him if he hadn't been with his father in the Underworld.

Dead, he thought. No way could he have lived with himself if he'd ever forced another to have intercourse with him. And, there is no doubt he would have denied himself to the point he became a danger. No. It's best to remain a secret. Computers, cars and indoor plumbing didn't mean humans weren't the same reactive creatures as hundreds of years ago.

raton watched Lia talk to the humans and had to admire her authority. It shouldn't be a surprise given her position as a police officer. In his experience few carried the air of confidence needed to truly lead others and make them listen without threat of violence.

There was something undeniable about someone that was able to tell another what they were doing wrong and have them listen without argument or justification. He was so used to those around him using power at times like this, but Lia did nothing of the sort.

She walked back to his side and he looked for signs that anything was off. All he saw were sexy curves and a beautiful woman. But there were no signs that she'd been infected by evil.

"So, what did your boss say?" A gasp left her, and she swiveled on her heels to stare at him with wide eyes. "Did you ask God about me and those shadows?"

The strangest things happened. The ever-present weight in his chest eased and an emotion he only felt when his sister was near filled his heart. Was he really happy? When one corner of his mouth lifted, he realized that he was indeed delighted by this female.

"No. I didn't talk to God. I spoke with the archangel Gabriel," he informed her. "He is in charge of the Warrior Angels."

"I cannot believe you spoke with an honest to God archangel about me. Wait. Why isn't Michael in charge of you guys? Wasn't he the one that lead the fight against Lucifer? Or does the Bible have it all wrong?"

A chuckle left Araton. The archangels were not a subject most humans had any real knowledge of. "Michael wanted a break from the fighting, so Gabriel took over. They'll change in a century or two. Raphael always seems to be the one in charge of everything."

"Got it. So, what did Gabriel say?"

Araton scanned the area. After Tristan and Slate finished with the human phones and Lia sent them home the street went pretty silent. Zander and the others ushered the supernaturals to the bar below the building they were next to.

"Gabriel said we need to keep an eye on you to make sure the darkness doesn't take hold in you and turn you."

Natalia started walking down the street while glancing all around them. It wasn't the same as the other night when they were at Jackson Square. Then she was vigilant. Now she seemed to be looking, but not really seeing anything.

"What did he say I would turn into? I'd rock horns, but I don't think grey is my color," she said. Her sarcasm punched him in the groin as if she were talking dirty to him.

Ignoring his arousal, Araton reminded himself that he was in New Orleans on a mission. At the moment, his mind added. "You will not turn into an actual demon. More that you will become evil and not care who and what you hurt as your emotions are destroyed piece by piece."

"Don't sugar coat it, Wings. I'm too stubborn to turn evil.

Let's scout the area and make sure there aren't any lingering demons nearby."

Araton fell into step beside her and was surprised how the mundane activity soothed his restlessness. "I'm not so sure stubbornness will stop demonic energy from taking over, but I believe if anyone can keep it at bay it's you, Dove."

They walked in silence for several minutes before Natalia pulled her phone from her back pocket and checked the screen. "I need to report for my shift. I will meet up with you later if you're around."

Araton ran his finger over her cheek and gazed into her stunning green eyes. "I will find you."

"Or you could give me your number so I can reach out if I see anything. I have Dante's cell programmed in, but I'd rather call you. You can teleport anywhere and be there faster than he can."

Araton stepped so close to Lia he could smell her sweet scent. "Is that the only reason you'd rather call me?"

Natalia swallowed then licked her lips while keeping her gaze on his mouth. "You're better looking. And saved my life with your blood. Doesn't matter that it was an accident. Having you inside me saved me in more ways than one."

"Not really," he murmured against her ear as he leaned toward her. "There's so much more I can give you."

Lia took a step away from him and fanned her face with her hand. "Damn, Wings. You've got game. It's a good thing I have to be on duty soon or I might do something I'll regret. Give me your number." He told her his cell number and she input the information.

"There will be no regrets when we come together," Araton told her before he went invisible. He lifted off into the air and hovered close by to watch as Lia looked all around searching for him. She gave up far too quickly for his liking.

There was no time to linger and watch the human. There were demons actively trying to summon Lucifer in the area. It was much harder to shroud himself in the hyper focus he'd always had.

He resolved to only do the job, but by the time he'd reached the rooftop he was already thinking of the sexy cop. Calling his weapon to his hand, Araton flew off in search of demons to slice and dice.

* * *

Araton watched from a rooftop as Lia left the station. He'd managed to kill a hellhound and three skirm before he returned to Zander and his Dark Warriors to check in and see how their patrol was going.

The fact that Izzy was walking the streets and had not yet been attacked was proof that she had acquired some type of protection or shield during her absence from the realm. As he had told Izzy twenty minutes ago. The shift might be because she matured.

No one really knew how her signature would change as she grew. Araton for one didn't believe the Goddess would leave Izzy vulnerable forever. It wouldn't make sense. The Goddess needed the Vampire Princess as much as the realm needed the Goddess.

A familiar smile caught his eye and he snapped to attention like a dog heeding a call. With her black hair in a tail on the back of her head, Natalia waved to a fellow officer and headed to her patrol car.

She was alone, making him wonder how she was doing after losing her partner. Not that they were the same type of partners as Orlando and Santiago. They didn't go to every scene together and didn't drive around in the same vehicle.

As Lia had explained they worked the same area and

never went into a dangerous situation without each other as back-up. They also spoke several times a night and crossed paths frequently.

It was when Araton recalled that she had no backup that he'd headed back to the station. And, no. That wasn't an excuse for him to return and see the female again. She was aware of the supernatural now and wouldn't hesitate to run headlong into a situation she wasn't equipped to deal with.

He'd seen her courage enough to know that she wouldn't hesitate. Her code of honor demanded that she eliminate any danger to her people. They had that in common. There was no way he would be able to ignore a demon if he encountered one.

He flew above the car and scanned the area while keeping an eye on her movements. The city was quiet, and the energy wasn't as Dark as it had been a few nights ago when he arrived.

What Araton found interesting was that there wasn't as much demonic activity in this city as there usually was. What action there was seemed to be highly concentrated in specific areas.

A car came speeding around a corner in front of Lia at a speed that caused the rear wheels to squeal. Immediately, the lights and sirens on the top of Natalia's car were on and she was taking off after the driver.

Araton's heart skipped a beat and he found himself taking off at top speed in the next second. Before he knew it, he was on top of the car. He managed to maintain his invisibility and he was in the air again when the car tried to turn right down an alley but didn't make it.

The loud sound of metal crashing into brick was loud in the night. Lia had her car parked and her gun drawn in the blink of an eye. Tapping on the glass with the end of the gun, Natalia called out, "Get out of the car with your hands up."

Several seconds passed and Araton nearly ripped the guy from his crumpled vehicle. Lia called for backup on her shoulder mic. The guy got out of the car and tried to take off down the alley.

Araton had landed and used a shield to hide his presence. The male slammed into it and fell on his ass. Natalia was on the offender's back and handcuffing him. Another cop car arrived and called something else into base before he got out of the car.

"I've got the perp under control," Natalia called out. "Can you get an ambulance, Wexler? And tow car for the vehicle?"

"Already done," Wexler told her as he shinned his light inside the passenger side window. "We've got paraphernalia." The other officer shone his light in the back.

Natalia hauled the guy up and pushed him toward the accident. Araton followed in their wake. An ambulance arrived and checked the offender over and gave him the all clear.

Lia shoved the offender in the back of her car and drove him back to the station while the other officer waited for the other car to be removed. Araton felt like a creepy stalker as he waited in the shadows for Natalia to return.

What the hell was he doing? He should be out searching for signs of demons, not hiding and waiting for a human female. It went against everything he stood for. He crouched down prepared to take off when Natalia's voice caught his attention.

It was a sign he was exactly where he needed to be. God rarely intervened, but every once in a while, He sent a sign telling them what to do. It was then that Araton recalled the shadows that flew right into Lia's chest. He had to keep an eye on her. If she went Dark on them, she could cause a significant amount of damage with her training and weapons.

Araton took to the skies and followed Lia once again. She seemed to be driving aimlessly throughout the Quarter for several minutes before she took off at a high speed. He followed and landed next to her vehicle when she stopped in front of store that looked closed.

"Jesus, Wings. You need to announce yourself. You nearly gave me a heart attack."

Araton couldn't help but smile at her admonition. "Always expect me to appear out of nowhere. It's how Warrior Angels operate. Even if we choose to show ourselves to humans. Besides, I'm trained for stealth. Calling out an alert would alert demons to my presence."

"Why are you here for a simple human theft?" She asked as she approached the building and glanced inside the plate glass window at the front. The interior was dark and appeared empty.

"I saw you and thought I would check in and see how the night is going," he admitted moving closer to her body.

"Pretty boring. No signs of demons or rogue supernaturals," she replied as she tested the door handle.

Araton made her pause when he touched her forearm. They stared at one another for several long minutes. Unable to resist any longer, Araton bent his head and shocked them both by lowering his face to hers. When his arousal blazed to life and started burning bright in his veins, he tamped it down and gentled his hold. Her pupils dilated as she stared back at him.

His lips brushed against hers, making the inferno threaten to run out of control. Need licked at his insides, making him ache for her body. Gently he moved his mouth over hers. Her reaction provoked him to let go for the brief seconds they had.

With a groan, he let go of her hands and tugged her uniform top from her pants. After pushing his way under the tight vest, he was finally able to place one big palm under her shirt on her lower back. His mind settled and rioted for more at the same time.

His tongue delved into her mouth when she gasped and held her close. Their tongues tangled wetly, sliding against each other for several heated seconds. When he finally broke the kiss, she was panting. He imagined her without the bullet proof vest on and wondered if her nipples were hard. He could practically feel them brush against his chest. Despite the layers that separated them, the contact tempted him like nothing else had in his long life.

She looked up and he became lost in her green eyes. It was stunning to realize he was affecting her. Of course, it was nowhere near as much as she was affecting him.

"I want more, but now is not the time for any of this," she told him honestly. "I let myself get carried away just now and I can't. I have a thief in this shop and we're standing here kissing."

It was a sobering moment, but it didn't stop Araton's cock from jerking inside his pants. "I'm not sure what came over me. I have never lost sight of a task as I did just now. I shouldn't have done that, but I can't bring myself to be sorry. You are the sexiest female I've ever met." His announcement made her cheeks flush as she glanced away.

"We will continue this later," she promised. "Seeing as sex is clearly on the table for angels. I wasn't sure."

"My brother Abraxos invented sex," Araton teased. "Angels are definitely big fans of the act. Although, my brothers would say I live to fight. That I'm impulsive and act without thinking."

"I look forward to seeing exactly how impulsive you can be...wait. There's movement. We will pick this up later," she promised.

It took a ton of effort to keep his mouth from hers and his

hands to himself. She drove him to the edge with need. When she headed to the back entrance, Araton followed. He kept his wings hidden and stayed far enough back that he wouldn't interfere with her job. He enjoyed watching her move silently through the night in her black uniform.

When she took off running, he initially increased his pace, but stopped when he didn't sense any malignant energy in the area. This was her job. A shout had him moving again. After several steps, the pop of a gun made him teleport.

When he reappeared in the courtyard in the middle of the businesses, he froze at the sight in front of him. Natalia was standing over the prone figure of a human male that was bleeding from a gunshot wound.

"What the fuck happened?" He demanded.

The look on her face when she glanced up at him was filled with horror and indifference. "He tried to run then pulled a weapon on me. I need to call this in."

A knot filled Araton's gut with dread. This wasn't Natalia. He didn't know her very well, but something assured him this wasn't how she would normally react. The question was what the cause of the dissonance was. And he didn't see any weapons near the body.

Natalia pressed the radio on her shoulder and called the incident in to her fellow cops and asked for emergency medical assistance. Araton thought that was a waste of time. The human was dead. And she had killed him.

"You do know your bullet killed him, right?"

Lia turned rapidly and glared at him. "Would you have rather allowed him to plunge that blade into my heart?" She growled the words and pointed to a silver glint he'd missed earlier.

Relief was sweet when it hit. The knife had fallen under the guy. He'd begun to believe she was starting to turn. "No. I wasn't sure if you should let whoever is on the other end of that radio know."

Shaking her head, sirens started blaring in the distance. "They will make the call. Not me. A ton of cops and medical personnel will be arriving any moment. There's always a chance they can save him. But you need to disappear," she told him.

He cupped her cheek and looked into her eyes. "I'll be right here. We have unfinished business."

Lia licked her lips, but her name being called out by responding officers interrupted the moment. Araton made himself invisible and wished he could ignore the fact that he heard her mutter under her breath. "He was going to kill me, right? There was nothing else I could do."

Once again Araton's blood went cold. It seemed Lia wasn't as confident as she portrayed. He was going to have to keep an eye on her.

CHAPTER 10

*L*ia ran a hand through her hair. She'd taken her ponytail down after returning to the station to deal with the aftermath of the shooting. She was exhausted and ready to sleep. And, looked like death warmed over. That could be the large bruise still on her cheek from the other night. Angel blood healed the worst of her injuries, but it hadn't gotten rid of that entirely.

"So, the perp came at you with his weapon raised above his head and you reacted to save your life," her Chief clarified as he read through her statement. "I shouldn't be surprised by the increase in violence. With this virus spreading faster than the doctors can deal with, everyone is on edge. Even my cops are trigger happy."

"What's that supposed to mean?" Lia snapped at Chief Williams.

Williams lifted his head and stared at her with narrow eyes. Anger bubbled just below the surface. First Araton questioned her actions and now her boss was. What did they want? For her to allow herself to be killed?! She reacted precisely like she was trained.

"I suggest you watch your tone. I know you're under stress and losing Turner has impacted you greatly. You were partners for lack of a better term. If you need to go home and get more rest, I will take you off the rest of your shift. I don't need IA up my ass because I had officers on duty that shouldn't have been there," her Chief told her.

It took more effort that she cared to admit to keep herself from raising her voice with Williams again. Several deep breaths later, she uncurled her fists and placed her palms on her thighs.

"I'm good. Tired yes, but nothing that's impeding my performance. I just need a cup of coffee and I'm good to go."

Williams lifted an eyebrow and stood up, signaling to her their meeting was done. "Don't be a martyr and overwork yourself. It will do you no good if you start making stupid mistakes. Only more paperwork."

"Yes sir," she replied with a forced smile. Lia walked to her desk and grabbed her tumbler and filled it with coffee then headed out the door. She hadn't been in her car for two minutes when she was called to a body that was found in a warehouse nearby.

Her heart started racing in her chest as she flipped her siren and lights on. Slowing as she approached the red light, she blasted through a second later when she was sure the coast was clear.

It had been months since she'd been called to a death in the business district. It was impossible not to wonder if it was the demons killing more people. Not that she'd been called to one scene involving the supernatural all night.

Now that she knew about their existence it was impossible to think about anything else. Especially after she'd been kissed by an angel. Araton was impulsive and took her by surprise with his kiss. Her lips still tingled from it, and her body ached for more.

A full body shiver made her feel like she was having a seizure the moment she turned down the street leading to the scene. Her mind screamed evil. If there were dead bodies, there was no doubt of something malicious at play. Even if it was just a matter of some homeless dying alone in a location they'd snuck into, it still qualified as cruel. Society should do better by its people. With that thought in mind she shut her sirens and lights off.

Lia contemplated calling for backup and decided on Araton rather than her fellow men in blue. She'd gone in after she'd input his digits and added the angel emoji. It made her chuckle to see the cute little figure. The real angel was so very different from the smiling peaceful image.

"What's wrong?" Araton barked into the phone after she pressed the icon for his number.

"There are so many ways I can answer that. But right now, I need you and your brothers at a warehouse on the east side. There are reports of at least one dead body and when I turned onto the street, I nearly crashed from the sensation of being suffocated," she admitted as she pulled to the curb in front of the location.

"A human should not be able to feel the presence of evil," Araton informed her.

"Thanks, Captain Obvious. I wasn't aware that this was a new and frightening sensation for me to have. I blame you for this by the way. With your angel blood running through my veins God only knows what I will feel next," she snarked and scanned the front of the building.

The place looked desolate and empty. She doubted it was used at all at the moment. The weeds growing up through cracks in the parking lot and the dirt covered window on the side attested to that.

"For your sake I hope you have my essence inside you deeper than those shadows." His comment was muttered low, making her wonder if he wasn't really speaking to her. Either way she ignored it. It was too tempting to reply with a double entendre.

"I don't see a sign of activity anywhere in the vicinity. Whoever called isn't here anymore, either," she told him as she got out of the car.

"That doesn't mean much. The demons and skirm could be inside. Stay on alert. We will be there soon." The sound of wings flapping told her he was flying as he spoke to her. How the heck did he manage to hold a conversation on his cell while flying?

"Okaaa…aah," she shouted when something hit the concrete next to her. Gun in hand, she had it poised to shoot while she turned to the side. "Fucking hell!" She screamed.

Araton lifted his head. The look on his face spoke of his thousands of years killing demons. It might have been the way his massive red wings extended out to the sides of his body. Or perhaps the flaming sword in his hand. It was the look of death on his face coupled with the wings and flaming sword, she decided.

Ayil and Abraxos landed a second later. "You enjoy taunting the human," Ayil told his brother. Lia couldn't tell if it was a recrimination or not.

Araton leveled a look at his brother. "Feel that? It's almost as strong as it was at that house the other night."

Abraxos who she thought of spending more time flirting was hyper-focused at the moment as he scanned the area. She sensed something the second she turned down the street, but it hadn't gotten any worse. In fact, she barely sensed anything now that she thought about it more.

Araton's warning about the evil energy seeping into her pores and changing her made her swallow bile. She wasn't turning, was she? The way he'd looked at her after shooting the guy behind the store flashed through her mind.

She wasn't about to try and talk to a perp that was threatening her with a knife. Sure, she had a gun. But that didn't mean his weapon wasn't potentially lethal. Her actions were warranted. The look on the guy's face told her he was going to kill her.

"Demons," Ayil and Abraxos said at the same time. "I'm calling Dante and Zander. The Dark Warriors can help deal with this scene," Ayil added.

Lia stepped forward and held up her hand. "Now, wait just a minute. We don't even know what we are walking into. My Chief will send backup if I don't report to him soon. Everyone knows I accepted a call here about a dead body. You can't make it disappear."

Araton shook his head. "We have no time for this shit. Demons could be getting away as we stand here and debate how this will be handled. I am going in."

Natalia ran after him when he moved to the entrance at a fast clip. "You can't just ignore me."

"You understand this is a matter of life and death, right? Shit won't stay calm for long where demons are involved. You should have learned that lesson," Araton called out to her as he continued without pausing.

They were close to the entrance and Lia was forced to lower her voice. "I get what's at stake here. You forget I'm the breakable one. I almost died once at the hands of demons. You're immortal and can't die."

Araton stepped close to her body with tension making him stand stiffly. "You will not be harmed on my watch. And, I can be killed. It's very difficult to manage, but no being is unkillable."

The fierce expression on his face told Lia he meant every word he said. She wasn't sure how that made her feel. She was used to taking care of herself. The guys she'd dated had never done much beyond dinner for her, and here was this sexy angel promising to make sure she wasn't hurt.

You're not dating him, Lia. Get your head on straight, woman. Grateful that she reminded herself of pertinent facts here, she focused on what she actually had an issue with. "All I'm asking is that we don't erase everything. I need to be able to call in detectives and the CSI team if they are called for."

Araton nodded and turned to enter the building. Ayil was hovering near a window high up on the building. He made some hand signals down to Araton and Abraxos. She had no idea what they were trying to say, but apparently it was the all clear because the angels had the door open and were through it before she knew it.

The scent of blood and rot blasted her in the face. Initially she couldn't see where the smell was coming from. It was too dark inside the warehouse. Her vision cleared in stages. First, she saw tall shelving units along the far wall. There seemed to be boxes stacked on some shelves. She withdrew her flashlight and shone it around the area, but the beam didn't reach very far.

Next, she noticed Araton and his brothers standing back to back as they scanned the area. Her light exposed debris on the floor. Mostly trash and a few metal parts. As her head moved around the space, she noticed there were stairs in one corner leading up to what looked like an office. The door was hanging precariously, and the windows were broken leaving only shards in the bottom of the frame.

When she glanced back at her angel, she saw what was at his feet and bile started rising like the tide up her throat. It didn't take much to figure out what the wet substance was on the floor. The lumps had a distinct human look to them. That was an arm, she thought.

As she moved closer, she realized it was actually a leg. A

torso with a pentagram carved into the flesh was tossed next to it. A noise behind her made her jump toward the brothers.

Araton and Ayil were in motion before she moved an inch. They flew in opposite directions while Abraxos stayed close. Snarling in Araton's direction sounded loud throughout the mostly empty building. The area was one massive room with remnants of machinery to one side and the shelving on the other. There might be a separate area in the back where Ayil had headed, but she couldn't tell.

She rolled her ankle when she stepped on something soft as she moved away from the violent noises. Red-orange flames swiveled through the air as Araton flew up a few feet in the distance. Something black and dog shaped leaped after him. The flaming sword slashed at the same moment and a loud screech was cut short when the demon died.

Able to look away after the body fell to the ground below Araton, Lia looked down and confirmed her suspicion she'd stepped on a limb. This time it was an arm. The beam of her light seemed to be glued to the gruesome sight.

She took a step away from what seemed to be a pile of bodies and pointed her beam around the shelves in front of her. "Are there anymore here?" Abraxos called out behind her.

She'd assumed they were going for quiet but realized how ridiculous that was given the noise now coming from Ayil's direction. "Not in this direction," Araton replied and landed beside her a second later.

"Do you need help, brother?" Araton shouted to Ayil.

"Fuck off," came the grunted response.

"What happened here?" She asked as she illuminated more of the area around them. Blood splattered on crumpled boxes and metal shelves. There was a large puddle about three feet from where the bodies were piled.

She wondered at the dismemberment. Typically, a body

was cut up for easier disposal. It was harder to identify remains if you couldn't find all the pieces. During the academy she'd learned about the few serial killers that ate their victims. Seeing the pieces laid out above the bloody pentagram told her why it was done in this warehouse.

"Another fucking ritual to call Lucifer," Araton spat.

"Did they succeed?" Lia blurted, suddenly very worried about having the Devil himself traipsing around her city.

"They might have," said a familiar voice with a heavy Scottish accent. The Vampire King came into view a second later. Dante, the Cambion Lord and his daughter were next to him.

"Word on the street is that Lucifer is possessing a human somewhere in the Quarter," Dante added as they all stopped a few feet away.

Izzy scanned the ground and swallowed thickly then met Lia's gaze long enough for her to see the Princess wasn't as hardened as Natalia originally believed. The horror was undeniable, regardless of how much anyone had seen.

What happened to these innocent people was abhorrent and she wanted to make sure no one else was harmed by these vile fucking demons. "How do we find out if he's out there killing in my city?" She demanded.

Araton lifted his wings as he walked toward the pentagram. "Before we get to that. We need to clear the worst of the scene but leave a body so Natalia can call in her colleagues. Humans were called here. There's no need to have you guys try to erase all traces from the police databases."

Lia glanced at her angel grateful he'd thought of what she needed to do here. The body parts and blood coupled with the smell would draw media attention and become national news even in the current climate. It would cause even more panic in her city.

Dante glanced around and pulled his phone from his back pocket. "I've called Aison and the others here to help deal with this. I will check with more of my contacts to the Underworld. It's possible archdemons are spreading lies to keep other, lower level demons in line. Shit has been chaotic since Crocell went off the path."

"Och, that bitch needs to leave our kids alone," Zander cursed. "You might be right about the rumor being false. Lucifer being on Earth is likely the only thing that will get through to her. No' that it will help. Lucifer will be far worse than having to keep her from taking our kids."

Lia had no idea what the Vampire King was talking about. She'd care that some crazy demon was hunting children, but he was right. If Lucifer was here that needed to be dealt with and fast.

"I don't think he will be able to maintain possession," Araton cut in. "He is bound to the Underworld. That will pull him back sooner rather than later."

"But he could find a way to break that bond before being pulled back," Abraxos added.

"You try and find more information, Dante. Let's comb through the…bodies here. We might be able to find clues as to who walked away from this massacre," Lia told them, refocusing the conversation.

"That's actually brilliant. I guarantee everyone here was wondering what spell they could use to get more information. We often think in terms of magic means that we forget the mundane," Izzy interjected.

Lia shrugged. "I haven't been part of this world long enough for it to come to mind. I don't want the devil running around on Earth, but I also don't want his demons here. Even if we don't find a clue leading us to Lucifer, we might find something to tell us where we can find this fucking nest of demons and get rid of them."

"We will find and destroy every demon in this city," Araton promised.

"I will destroy them," Izzy interjected with a snarl. Lia glanced at her then at her father. Surely, he wouldn't allow her to face demons. He seemed like he was overprotective of her. Always standing close and watching the area around them.

"Isobel was born with certain powers from their Goddess," Araton explained. "One of them is the ability to kill an archdemon with a touch. And when she kills them, their souls are destroyed. There is no getting back in line for another body and another chance like usual."

"You're telling me these beasts will come back even if we kill them? And, this woman makes sure they don't get that chance?" That was nearly impossible for her to wrap her mind around.

"Aye," Zander answered as he stood a bit closer to his daughter. "She is the only weapon capable of delivering true death to a demon."

Aison and several other of the Dark Warriors she met arrived at that second which was good. Lia couldn't wrap her mind around what she'd discovered in the past hour. From arriving to find the abattoir in the warehouse to the fact that Izzy could kill archdemons with a touch. And, none of that was as important as them finding out if Lucifer was walking around inside someone else's body. Time to get to work.

CHAPTER 11

ante's skin crawled as he walked into The Underground. Not the most unique name, but then again neither was his favorite haunt. That being Zakara's old place, Seven Lively Sinz. That joint had character, and she'd done a good job of keeping the violence to a minimum.

Dante rarely frequented places like this because he didn't want to associate with full demons like his father. Unfortunately, incubus and succubus were often found at the demon run clubs because they liked violent sex. The kind that created a scene and left bodies for human law enforcement to be called to deal with.

Not many supes that Dante knew of wanted the humans to learn of their existence. Hayden, the Omega of the shifters was the exception to that rule. And, that had to do with him being tired of keeping the demons at bay and protecting innocents that did nothing to help their cases.

The scent of Brimstone filling the air made Dante's heart race and sweat bead on his brow. His worst fucking nightmares came from his time in Hell. Rhys was a lucky sonofabitch to have such an outstanding memory from the Underworld after finding his angelic mate during a mission there. But, Dante didn't need the physical punch in the gut today. Shit was hitting the fan in the city and Zander was freaking out about the lack of demons hunting his daughter.

Dante understood. Before she returned from Khoth they couldn't take their daughter out to get an ice cream without being attacked. Hell, they couldn't even keep her at home safely which is why they took her to the dragon realm.

No one told him specifically what happened to the Princess, but Dante knew the reason for the trauma in her eyes. He'd worn it himself countless times when he lived in the Underworld. And, he'd seen it countless times on victims throughout his life. He'd made it his mission to help victims recover from sexual assault and had been doing it for centuries. He was tempted to offer Isobel an ear but didn't think it would help much. There was more to her story and he wasn't about to push her to talk about it.

Watching a Daeva demon flirt with an incubus at a table in the corner, Dante sucked it up and headed to the black bar in the middle of the room. Just like Kara's old bar, the Underground had too many years of blood, booze, and slimy green goo covering the tabletops and floors to be wiped clean.

"What'll it be?" The grizzled barkeep asked. The male was likely a Melcom demon. He was tall which only highlighted his slim stature. Like most of his kind, he had a weasel-like face.

The demon made a good bartender. He was able to intimidate with a look and a scent. The pheromones he was throwing off had an edge to it that had Dante's teeth on edge. His scowl said he was more likely to poison you than anything else. It almost made Dante hesitate to ask for a drink.

But Dante knew better than to judge a demon based on

its appearance. The most attractive could kill you while they fucked you, and the ugliest could give you the shirt off their back. For a price, of course. Dante had always judged others based on their actions. Rarely did he find a demon's actions spoke to a compassionate personality.

"Vodka rocks. I need a drink after the latest rumors," Dante replied.

"What rumors would that be? There's always bullshit being said by someone somewhere. If it's about demons being responsible for that human virus going around that's total bullshit."

Dante chuckled and gave the male some cash for his drink. "That's too tame for us. We like to get up close and personal. I don't think the four horsemen have escaped the seventh circle. It's that Lucifer is finally on Earth."

It seemed as if silence descended on the bar at his announcement, making him regret coming here. "What the fuck do you know?" A male growled at his back.

Years of training had Dante on his feet and slamming the males head into the bar in the blink of an eye. Never leave an enemy at your back and never show weakness. The incubus struggled under his hold, but Dante kept him pinned by the shoulders.

The glass of vodka he hadn't even sipped had been spilled and the glass clattered to the floor where it shattered. Stepping on the shards, Dante got in the male's face. "I know a lot more than you, asshole. You got a problem?"

"No," the incubus replied after studying Dante's face for several tense minutes. "We've all been waiting to see if it's true."

Dante let the male go and signaled for another drink. "I'd like to know who started the bullshit to begin with. Humans can't contain his power. It would destroy them within minutes."

"You're right about that," the incubus agreed. "Can I get a beer, Dion. We all assumed Lucifer would be inside a supernatural or a half-breed like yourself. But no one believed the supes would give their bodies up for possession."

Dante paid for his second drink and took a sip then shook his head. "You're right about that. Those fuckers are pretentious fucks. It's a bullshit lie."

The Daeva demon that had been flirting with the incubus leaned against the bar in front of Dante. "It's not a lie. We've been performing rituals all over town the past few nights. Many were killed by those Dark Warriors, but they couldn't be everywhere at once. One of them was bound to work."

"You smell like blood, fear and death. So, your ritual failed then?" Dante threw out at her to get a reaction. All of it was true. She reeked and if her efforts paid off then she wouldn't be in a bar without Lucifer.

"Fuck you, half-breed. It wasn't my fault the angels showed up and ruined everything. He will know that," she professed, but he could see the doubt in her eyes. Lucifer wasn't very forgiving. He'd kill her if he thought she didn't try hard enough.

"He sure will," the incubus agreed and ran a hand over her shoulder while releasing some pheromones of his own. Bile churned in Dante's gut with the scent from his nightmares. "Let's go back to our booth." The female nodded and the pair walked away leaving Dante alone at the bar.

Once the tension had dissipated the rest of the patrons returned to their drinking and whatever else they were doing. Dante refused to look too closely. He had no desire to get that familiar with anyone in the joint.

He hadn't gotten confirmation of Lucifer's return, but he knew where they needed to focus now. Killian could help send out an alert on T-Rex asking for anyone to report a missing friend or relative.

Life had become decidedly not fun. Ever since Nikko had been killed Dante had taken on more responsibilities within the Alliance. He didn't mind. He actually enjoyed it, but it left little time for sex which was necessary for him to continue living.

Not that he could blame his diminished activity on his duties. Dante was tired of unfulfilling sexual encounters. For years he watched those around him find their Fated Mates.

He'd never before considered how much that impacted someone's life until he watched his friends' lives transform to something beyond happy. Complete was the word that came to mind. Something he was not.

* * *

Lia groaned as she rolled over. Her head was pounding and her back ached. What the hell did she drink last night? She didn't recall drinking at all, but there was no denying the killer hang over beating her down at the moment.

She threw an arm over her closed eyes to shield them from the bright sun that seemed to find its way through her closed curtains. Of course, it was intent on blinding her. That's what happened when you were hung over.

Wait. What the fuck was that? She sat up and had to catch herself as she nearly fell back down. Her hand landing on a sharp rock confirmed what her eyes told her in that brief blurry second. She wasn't in her bedroom.

Her heart raced and her mind scrambled to make sense of what she was seeing as she jumped to her feet. Bile churned in her stomach and she doubled over as she looked around.

How the hell did she get outside? In the middle of the bayou. Grassy fields surrounded her, and in the distance there was a swampy shore. Blood and dead animals surrounded her.

Her hand flew to her mouth as she noticed the symbols and pentagram. She turned her head and lost the battle with her stomach. Her last snack of carrots right before her shift ended the night before made a return trip as she threw up.

When she went to wipe her mouth with the back of her hand, she forced her arm out to the side. The blood on her skin was what made her lose the contents of her stomach in the first place.

She tiptoed to the swamp and plunged her hands into the murky water. It wasn't the cleanest location to wash up, but no way was she leaving the substance on her hands. She didn't even care if an alligator surged from the water and grabbed hold of her. She deserved the death roll.

A glance over her shoulder confirmed that thought. The mess of bodies was bigger than she could believe. Had she done all of this? She had no recollection but was covered in the evidence.

The water smelled foul as she splashed it on her face. No matter. She had no idea what her face looked like but given the smears all across her dark grey t-shirt and sweats that she wore to bed last night she'd guess she was a bloody mess.

She even tugged off her shirt and tried to wash it in the swamp. Giving up on that she scanned further out from the mess she'd woken up in the middle of and tried to determine where exactly she was at.

There were countless swamps within a couple hours of the city. And she wasn't familiar with many of them. All she heard were birds and insects for miles. With no other choice, she searched the site where the ritual had very obviously taken place for her cell phone.

She didn't recall driving out here and couldn't see her car. And, she sure as hell didn't remember killing and cutting up all the animals. There was no weapon nearby either. None of this made any sense. She had no shoes or socks on and yet her feet weren't cut up or blistered as if she had walked there from her house in the city.

It was impossible that she traveled so far unless she somehow developed wings and flew there. Who knew what the angel blood had done to her? Reaching over one shoulder she patted around but didn't find any signs of shit coming out of her back. Araton's words came back to her about the dark stuff surging into her body at the LaLaurie Mansion.

"Gabriel said we need to keep an eye on you to make sure the darkness doesn't take hold in you and turn you."

Is that what happened? Was she now evil? The answer to that was a resounding yes if she had killed all of these animals. Her head throbbed and her chest twisted with regret.

She wasn't going to get answers standing here. There was a possibility she would find a home and a phone, so she started walking away from the water. Rocks and sticks cut up her feet within minutes confirming she was right about the fact that she hadn't walked all the way out there.

The sun rose as she walked, and the day quickly heated to boiling. She continued for so long she doubted she was going in the right direction. Who would she call if she found a house? Her dad or one of her brothers?

No fucking way. She was not going to involve them in this nightmare. She had no idea how to reach Aison or Dante and wouldn't want to if she could. The only one she trusted was Araton.

Making her way through a patch of trees while trying to avoid the branches on the ground, Lia tried to recall her angel's phone number. Her angel? Since when had he become hers? From the moment they met, she realized. She'd been thinking of him as hers since the beginning but hadn't realized it until now.

It wasn't all that surprising given how sexy he was. Not

that she would ever know what it would be like to be with him. No way would he touch her with a ten-foot pole after what she had done. Something so pure shouldn't be with someone tainted by evil.

If she had another choice, she wouldn't even call him, but there wasn't anyone else she trusted. She was glad she'd tried to wash her shirt since the damp material cooled her off as she the day got hotter and sweat poured from her body.

She'd put the top on inside out to hide the blood stains. Thankfully, she got dirty and that managed to mask much of the blood from her pants. The last thing she wanted was to walk up to a random house covered in gore. It was animal blood, but it didn't make her feel any better about waking up the way she had.

The sun was high in the sky before she saw a house in the distance. Picking up speed, she ran the rest of the way, not caring that her feet got cut up in the process. Knocking on the door, she pushed her black hair from her face.

An older man answered the door. His eyes widened and he pushed through the screen door right away. "Why, you look like you've had quite the day. Where's you come from, cher?" His Cajun accent was thick, but his demeanor reminded her of home and for the first time in hours her body relaxed.

"I was left in the bayou a ways back and need to call a friend for help," she told him with as much honesty as she could.

"I'm going to call the Sherriff so he can investigate whoever hurt you. I won't bother asking questions. He'll want the information anyway."

Lia lifted her left foot to check the sharp pain in the bottom while shaking her head. "No. I'm a police officer in New Orleans. I need to get back to my Chief. He will take care of matters," she told the man.

"I can't imagine what kind of trouble your job brought you, but since you're a cop I will leave it to your department to handle. But you have to promise to let me know if I'm in danger out here. I lost my Maggie last year and it's just me now. My son worries about me."

"You're safe. Don't worry. This was because of a case I have been investigating. But I promise to make sure there are no suspects out here to cause problems."

"Thank you," he told her and went into his house. She waited on the porch for him to return.

"I figured you could use some sweet tea. And here's the phone."

"You're a true hero. Thank you," she told him and accepted both. She took a long drink then dialed what she hoped was Araton's number. If she was wrong she would call her dad.

"This is Araton," her angel growled into the phone.

A sob escaped her before she could stop herself. Very aware of the man watching her, she stopped the tears from falling. "It's Lia. I need your help. I woke up in the bayou with no knowledge of how I got there. I think it has something to do with that case I was investigating at LaLaurie Mansion. Can you come get me?"

"Lia? What the fuck? Where are you?" He demanded.

She asked the gentleman helping her where she was then told Araton who said he would be there soon with help. A second later he started walking up the driveway with his brothers.

All three of them wore black leather pants and a black top. Their wings were hidden, and she almost wished they'd left them out. She felt like there was a dark presence in her. Every time she tried to pinpoint the origin it eluded her. It might just be because of what Araton told her before. The only thing she knew for sure was that she didn't feel like she would be overrun by evil when he was with her.

"Natalia," Araton murmured when he saw her.

"Damn. You arrived fast. Were you nearby?" The guy asked.

"We are able to travel faster than most," Araton started, but Lia cut him off and said, "Privileges of being a cop, you know. Thank you so much for your help. We will patrol and make sure no one is in the area. You will be safe here."

Abraxos and Ayil nodded with Araton. "We will make sure of it."

The four of them turned and headed down the gravel driveway. She hadn't taken three steps before strong arms wrapped around her and she was lifted into Araton's hold.

"You have injuries on your feet," he explained.

Emotion overwhelmed her that second and tears filled her eyes. Lowering her head she admitted, "I think I might be evil."

One of Araton's fingers touched her chin and he encouraged her to lift her head. When she looked up, she saw heat in his. "You are not evil. I have no idea what happened, but under the dirt and grime I can see blood. If you got out here without memories of how there are demonic forces at work. That doesn't mean it is you, though."

She briefly told them everything that had happened since she opened her eyes including every detail from the blood to the animals to the symbols.

"We will investigate the scene where she woke up while you take her home," Ayil said.

"I woke up southeast from here," she told them. "I didn't have anything to tell me the exact location, but it was that direction." She pointed the way she came from.

"What do you think it could be?" She blurted before any of them could take off into the sky.

Araton paused with his wings now on full display. They were far enough from the house that they couldn't be seen by the old man that had helped her. "I'm not certain. I saw hints of darkness when you killed the thief, but I do not feel any malevolence in you now. I think we need to ask a magic user for help figuring this out so this doesn't keep happening to you."

"Are you thinking the Rowan sisters?" Abraxos asked.

"Pema and Isis are still in Khoth," Ayil said.

"Then we go to Marie Leveau," Araton told them. "Right now you guys gather what information you can, and I will take her home."

"Marie Leveau? Like the Voodoo Queen?" She asked.

"That's the one. She will have a spell or potion or talisman that will tell us if you have been infected," Araton explained.

She nodded. "Just promise you will kill me if we discover the demons took me over. I don't want to hurt anyone."

"It's not going to come to that," Araton promised.

Lia let it go for now and wrapped her arms around his neck. She held tight when he took off from the ground. She knew he made her invisible which was good. She buried her head in the crook of his neck and allowed the tears to fall. She might not make it out of this one alive. She wasn't going to live if she was evil now.

$\mathcal{A}$raton cursed as he and his brothers were forced to land. They'd flown out to the location Zander had told them about when they hit the invisible wall. He was hoping to be able to fly directly to the front door, but the Voodoo Queen was having none of that.

"Look," Ayil blurted as he pointed at tiny, winged faeries flying around what looked like an enchanted willow. The creatures were from the Unseelie court. Araton knew the powerful female had alliances with many creatures throughout the realm.

It shouldn't surprise him that she had an agreement with the Unseelie. They were often thought of as the dark and evil side of the Fae, while the Seelie were seen as the light and good. Araton had seen enough to know that was total bullshit. Yes, Cyril, the Unseelie King was a complete fucking jackass that was trying to take over Khoth.

Araton had seen the Seelie Queen a couple times but had never had any dealings with her. The few Fae he'd interacted with proved that they were all capricious, self-centered creatures.

"Her house is that way," Araton said as he pointed in the direction they needed to travel. "What in God is that smell? It smells worse than rotting demon."

"That Eau de Swamp Ass," Abraxos chuckled as they continued at a fast clip. Araton patted his pockets for the stones and salt Zander had given them.

He couldn't stop thinking of the scene his brothers described to him. There was no sign in the swamp that Lia had driven or even walked there. Her retreating footsteps were the only things visible. None of it made sense. How and why had she gotten there?

The three of them stopped at an old abandoned dock that was barely afloat in the murky swamp. The mist and fog were as thick as pea soup near the water's edge.

Araton recalled Zander telling him one scratch or bite from a Wendigo and they could become flesh-eating zombies. None of them were certain angels could be turned into flesh eating parasites, but he wasn't taking any chances. That was only the first obstacle. After passing the Wendigo they'd encounter Wraiths. They could not be destroyed and could devour them in the blink of an eye.

The bayou had a sound all its own that made Araton's jaw clench with anger that the sexy human with a heart of gold and spine of steel had been dumped in the middle of a blood sacrifice. If he forgot what happened to her, he could almost appreciate it as the crickets chirped and frogs croaked while crocodiles rippled through the water.

When he first arrived at the house to pick up a distraught Lia he'd fallen in love with the scene. The house was surrounded by trees where moss and lichen waged a battle that created a beautiful tableau with dappled sunlight filtering through the boughs. Here he saw more lichen and moss along with mud. Not as appealing as the house had been.

The knee-high grasses tangled around his legs. Araton growled as they finally made it to the old dock. It looked like it was ready to collapse, but Araton wasn't worried about that. He contemplated if they could fly across to the house he saw in the distance.

Lifting into the air he realized he could hover a few inches above the water but no higher. "Let's fly and avoid the boat," he suggested to his brothers.

Zeke's mate had given someone a crystal to call the boat to them, but that seemed like far too much work.

"Sounds good to me," Ayil agreed.

They took to the air a second later and hadn't made it more than three feet when movement on the banks caught Araton's attention. "We have company. Looks like they're the Wendigo we were warned about. I think we're immune to their bite or scratch, but let's not take any chances."

The sound of flames crackling in the night air prompted Araton to call his weapon to his hand. The orange glow was comforting in the dark night. The crackle added to the cacophony of the night.

Clouds cleared and the moonlight highlighted the zombie-like creatures' glowing, yellow-brown eyes. Araton's stomach rolled when he noticed the green slime dripping from their fangs. A quick glance told Araton there were easily fifteen or more of these creatures. Their sheer number was evidenced as the grass and water sizzled and popped where their slime hit.

Clothing hung in tatters on their bodies and through tears in their shirts, scales of a vibrant orange were visible. There were also green pustules that oozed from large sores that covered what he could see of their bodies.

"God that's vile," Abraxos complained. Araton had to agree. The smell of decaying flesh nearly made him toss his dinner.

"What did they say about these things?" Ayil asked.

"Aside from the fact that they might turn you into a flesh-eating zombie, don't be fooled be their sluggish movements," Araton explained. Zander told them that their lumbering gait was designed to lull victims into false complacency.

Long brown claws flared and nearly locked around his ankle. The sound of heavy door hinges groaning in the wind startled him and made him flinch. Thankfully, he'd pulled up his legs while he was trying to figure out where the noise came from. It was their version of a growl.

"That's more annoying than it is scary," he complained as he swung his weapon and sliced the head from its shoulders. The creature caught fire at the same time the water sizzled as blood hit. The stench was enough to peel paint off walls.

"These are some ugly mother-fuckers. They hit every branch on the way down and landed in a pile of feces," Abraxos added.

That seemed to kick them into gear and the rest moved swiftly, sending the crocs, toads and other swamp critters scurrying for safety. Water rippled and splashed against the Wendigo. Araton thought it'd clean the fuckers but it didn't touch the disease clinging to them. Claws reached for them while Araton let loose a battle cry that hopefully reached Marie's ears. That female had pretty tight security. He was surprised she managed to make any alliances. You had to be pretty fucking determined to get through this shit and not turn tail to run.

Araton swung his sword, easily decapitating the first to reach them. His brothers were right there with him in this fight. He expected the flaming sword to deter at least some of them. Most beings were afraid of their weapons of Light. It was a painful way to die. Unfortunately, it didn't seem to faze them at all.

There seemed to be an unrelenting wave of the fuckers as

he swung his sword. It was difficult to fly up or over to avoid the blood splatter. The only good thing was their flames seemed to incinerate most of the cast off.

"Abraxos," he called out as he saw one of them almost to his brother's legs. Without needing to look, he swung his weapon behind him knowing his inattention would be taken advantage of. The scream was music to his ears. A quick glance over told him he managed to kill another one.

Abraxos turned and sliced into the one at his feet. Ayil was in front of their brother. He saw the hit coming and couldn't move fast enough. Claws embedded into Ayil's lower wing. His brother's scream was loud enough he worried it reached Ayil's mate, Kennex. The female would geld Araton if he let anything happen to Ayil.

Araton ducked as Abraxos swung his weapon, sending an orange, pus-filled arm flying. The limb flopped around the sizzling water while Araton reached Ayil's side.

"Fuck," Ayil bitched and nearly fell into the water. "I need to land before I fall into that cesspool."

Araton was about to tell his brother to continue but a sudden sharp burn lanced up through his leg. Looking down he saw that he'd gotten too close to the water and the detached arm had clawed him. "Dammit. Watch the severed limb carries their poison. It got me."

"Go on Ayil," Abraxos ordered. "We will finish the last few and meet you on the end of the dock."

"Don't get too close to the house or you will incite the Wraith," Araton reminded him.

The demon that created these flesh-eating beings was devious. Being infected by a dead limb no longer attached to a body was the epitome of dedicated. How the hell did Marie Laveau control them? They were single-minded creatures that he couldn't see following instructions. Perhaps she really was the Goddess of Voodoo.

Araton renewed his efforts to eliminate the rest of the Wendigo. He slashed and slayed, leaving a smoldering pile in the bubbling water. Abraxos stayed close to his side while Ayil flew to the dock not far away.

When there were only a few left, Araton shoved his sword through the abdomen of one of the beasts and sent his energy through the sword. He felt his vitality draining into his weapon and was worried for a second he should have sliced fast. He wanted to see if he could eliminate them faster.

A second before he was going to remove his weapon and slash through the body, light flared and the being exploded. Araton put on a burst of speed and raced away from the gore.

His leg felt like lead, but he managed to stay in the air and reach Ayil a second later. "Salt," he announced as he reached into his pocket and pulled the satchel out.

"This shit isn't healing," Ayil told him when he poured some into his hand. "Somehow I don't think Kennex will want to sleep with a flesh eating angel."

"She'd love you no matter what you become," Araton told his brother suddenly wondering what that was like. Before meeting Natalia he'd never given it a second thought. Now, he found himself wanting that. With Lia. First, he had to ensure they all survived in one piece and that she was going to be okay.

Araton bent down and slapped his palm over the wound on his brother's wing. Ayil arched his back and shouted. The area had turned black and was rotting from the inside out. It was a good fucking thing he took the salt.

Abraxos took the salt from him and repeated the process on Araton's lower leg. He managed not to scream, but his clenched his jaw tight enough to crack teeth. Pain wracked him for what seemed like an eternity.

The only thing that brought him a measure of comfort for those long seconds was thinking about the kiss he and Lia had shared. Soon, Araton felt the barbs of black magic from the Wendigo venom leave his blood and the fire began to cool.

Araton looked up and noticed the Wraith watching them. "Zander gave us these magic stones. When I throw them we will need to move fast. We only have seconds to get to the door."

"Got it," Ayil replied as he extended his wing testing the injury. It seemed to move just fine. Araton pulled his arm back and let the stones go while yelling the spell he'd been taught.

The sudden shriek told Araton that the wraith was blinded. But there was no mistaking the creature's anger. Araton watched as the rocks hit their mark. Less than a second later, an eerie silence descended over the bayou. He didn't even hear the sounds of the animals and bugs anymore.

Araton moved at supernatural speed toward the house that looked like it was one windstorm away from falling into the disease riddled swamp. Abraxos's knuckles were rapping on the door within a millisecond while Araton was reaching for the handle to barge into the place.

"There's no reason to piss of the deadly female. If she's got these creatures out here there's no telling what she's capable of," Abraxos warned.

"I don't give a fuck. We need to get in there and get answers now," Araton replied. It was impossible to calm his need. Every second that passed was one that Lia was in danger. He knew whatever was happening to her was related to what happened at the LaLaurie Mansion. Both the night he met her and the next day.

Just as he was going to push his way inside, the door

creaked open. The entry way was empty as he and his brothers entered. Where was the powerful female? The door slammed shut the second they had crossed the threshold.

He watched as hundreds of black candles flared to life illuminating the place better than a fluorescent light. From the outside, the cottage appeared much smaller. He should have suspected there was a dimensional spell at work. No way could the female live in a home the size of his bathroom. She'd need space to brew her potions. He'd seen the setup at the Rowan sisters house. They had jars upon jars of ingredients throughout their kitchen.

Marie's home was one massive open area that was more cluttered than her shop on Bourbon Street. He laughed when he saw shrunken heads and dolls on one set of shelves. His nose started itching within minutes of being in room. It had to be the cloying sweet incense that permeated the air.

Abraxos touched a jar and chuckled. "She's got chicken feet and eyeballs. Seems cliché to me." There were also skulls of some kind. Nearby he thought he saw the embryos of various species.

Araton looked around for the powerful female and thought she could be standing right there but it would be hard to tell from all the antique bookshelves and sideboards with miniature skeletons and masks. The shear amount and variety of magical paraphernalia that surrounded them was astounding.

He looked for stairs or doors but found none. He didn't even see any hallways and the only place to sit was a velvet-covered armchair set before a blazing fireplace. Abraxos bumped into some jars, making Araton turn his head. If he broke something they might be killed, and their wings harvested.

"Watch it, asshole," Araton warned.

"Yeah. Dat is hard to git," said a female. Araton spun

around again and noticed the regal female sitting in the maroon chair. She wore a tignon of vibrant gold and an elaborate headdress that was adorned with numerous rubies, sapphires, emeralds, and diamonds. Most of her hair was stuffed under a wrap, but Araton saw a few black strands falling out.

Her creamy café-au-lait skin glowed right before a pulse of her power exploded out of her and nearly knocked Araton off his feet. Marie adjusted the luxurious gold and red shawl around her shoulders and smiled at Abraxos who never showed a sign of being affected by the blast.

"Ah. It's lovely to meet you, Marie. I'm Abraxos and these are my brothers," his brother crooned and picked up her small hand in one of his. Bending, Abraxos kissed the back of it then he shot her a smile that usually had females dragging him to their beds.

"Forgive our intrusion, but we have a matter of utmost importance and we need your assistance," Abraxos continued.

"Dere's always a life and death mattah with you warriors," she retorted in a heavy Cajun accent. There was no denying her message. She was telling them she had no patience for matters that didn't have anything to do with her and they were in her territory and she tolerated their presence but would take them out if necessary.

"With all due respect, this will affect you if Lucifer isn't stopped," Araton barked at the female.

Abraxos held up his hand. "What my brother is trying to say is that demons have been conducting countless rituals to free Lucifer from the confines of Hell. Rumor has it that he has possessed someone on Earth and is not long from being released of the spells that bind him to the Underworld. We were at one such location and black shadows separated from the walls of the house and surged into a human colleague."

"Where did dis happen?"

"It was at the LaLaurie Mansion," Araton added as he tried hard to reign in his temper. "All of our attempts to cleanse the space have failed."

"You clearly don' know da depth of dark dat is in da place. If there is anywhere dat will be powerful enough to release Lucifer from da chains dat bind him 'tis dat house. What will you give me for da potion to clean da space?"

"We will give you a city that is free of the worst fallen angel in existence," Araton growled at her. "If he is able to become corporeal, he will destroy you and all of your people."

"I'm no' witout powers angel. I can protect my own. But your God's human pets cannot."

Abraxos glared daggers at Araton before smiling at Marie. "What would be fair for your assistance?"

"Dere are many ghosts trapped in dat house. I can't help dem cross over. You help dem and give me some of your red feathers and I will give you what you need."

"Deal," Abraxos blurted and reached over his shoulder to tug several feathers from his wings. Holding them up, he said, "What do we need?"

Marie got up in a swish of fabric and walked to the kitchen area. She grabbed at least a dozen different jars and a large mortar and pestle. Adding pinches of this and that, she focused on her work as she spoke. "Spread dis around da house with a concentration over any sigils at da site of da ritual. Den you have your angels call up da spirits at da same time. When dey cross over you light the sigils on fire. You must do dis on da full moon."

"Do you have anything for the human infected by the darkness?" Araton asked, his tone much more subdued and almost pleading now. He even reached over his shoulder and pulled out some feathers. "I will give you some of my feathers. We need to help her. She's being transported to ritual sites while she sleeps."

"Dere is nothing I have dat will help dis woman. You must bring her to me," Marie told him. "Unless she dies first den you must burn da body."

"She won't be dying," he snarled while his chest moved like a bellows. It was impossible to calm his shit down enough to think straight. "Is there a safer way for us to reach you? Lia will not survive your Wendigo. I will not place her at risk," Araton informed the Voodoo Queen with no room for debate.

"You will bring her to my tomb in three days at noon," Marie told him then poured the concoction into a large jar. That was the day of the full moon when they had to use the potion on the mansion. "Now leave before I regenerate my Wendigo."

"Thank you," Abraxos said as he accepted the jar. Ayil grabbed hold of Araton and dragged him to the door before he could start yelling at her that they didn't have days. That Lia didn't have days. No matter how hard he tried to fight their current situation, he had a sinking feeling he was going to lose Natalia before he was able to help her.

The female was strong and determined to do what was right for others without consideration for herself. Natalia's inner light was a gift to the world. Darkness would descend if she was lost in the battle against evil. Marie Leveau had better have an answer for them or Araton would rain hell on demons.

$\mathcal{A}$raton scanned the houses and yards below him as he flew throughout the city. Countless colorful houses passed by below with quaint, quiet gardens. Nothing pinged his senses despite his desperate need for any sign of demons.

Natalia had disappeared from her bedroom an hour ago and he hadn't been fast enough to follow her. He'd naively assumed she was confined by mortal means of transportation.

Never in his wildest dreams did he believe she could teleport like upper level demons or angels. The fact that he was able to go anywhere with a thought mocked him at the moment. There was no way to go to individuals or he would have found his sister the moment she'd been taken a century before.

No way could he tolerate the thought of her suffering like Illianna had during her captivity in the Underworld. Not that he was happy about what his sister went through. He was murderous most days and on the bad days when he couldn't let go of his colossal failure where Illianna was concerned he went nuclear, killing hundreds of demons in his wake.

His trip to Marie Leveau had paid off, but he had to wait to implement anything for a couple more days. Patience wasn't his thing. Action was where he excelled. He was even better at killing shit.

None of them knew what happened to Lia when she disappeared like this. The last time this happened to her she called him from out near the swamps covered in blood. There had been dead animals near where she woke up but what he hadn't had the heart to tell her was not all the blood on her was from animals.

He couldn't stand to see her Light dim like it would if she suspected she had killed someone, or more than one person. Something pure shone from Natalia and made the world a better place. As an angel Araton was familiar with goodness on a level few really understood.

Ringing interrupted his search and had him stilling and hovering in the air above some quiet houses on the west side. Pulling his cell phone from his back pocket he nearly fell from the sky when he saw Lia's name flash on the screen.

Thumbing the screen, Araton tried hard to reign in the emotions battling in his mind. "Lia? Are you okay? What happened?" He barked sounding far angrier than he actually was.

"I...I don't know," she said on a sob. "The last thing I remember is going to the kitchen to make a drink after I showered. I had just slid my cell phone into the side pocket of my leggings and then I woke up here..." her words broke off as she choked and cried.

"Listen to me, Dove," he replied, gentling his voice and keeping the anger raging through his veins out as much as he could. He wasn't mad at her, but at Lucifer and his minions.

"Don't look around. Getting upset could attract any demons near you to your location."

"Okay," she said with a hiccup. "Can you come get me?"

"Where are you?" he asked.

"I'm at the University. Close to the water, I think. At least it looks like water out the window," she told him.

"The University of New Orleans?" He clarified. He was on the opposite side of the city searching through Marigny. He'd been over the Seventh Ward and Bayou St. John but hadn't gone to the University. He expected her to be closer to her house in Mid City.

"Yes. I don't know what building I'm in. There's blood…" Her voice cut out when he teleported to the campus. It didn't take long for him to home in on her location.

"I'm here, Dove," he told her, cutting off what she was saying. He didn't want her to focus on what surrounded her. Accessing his texting app, he shot a message to his brothers asking for them and the Dark Warriors to deal with what he thought would be the scene of at least one murder inside the Fine Arts building.

Not bothering with the door, he teleported inside and stopped short at the sight of Natalia standing there covered in blood. There was no sight of a body anywhere close, but he wasn't going to stick around with her. The others could do a search and deal with whatever they found.

Lia ran to him and he caught her up as she threw herself in his arms. "OhmyGodIthinkIkilledsomeone," she rushed out when he wrapped her up.

Araton tightened his hold and ran one hand down her back. "You're okay now. I won't let anything happen to you. Slow down and tell me again."

Lia took a deep breath and put some space between their bodies then wiped her eyes with the back of one hand smearing blood across her face. "I think I killed someone. We have to look around. Maybe they're not dead and we can help them."

"My brothers are going to be here…right now," Araton told her as he felt them arrive. A second later Ayil and Abraxos appeared next to them.

"Brother," Ayil greeted as he looked around.

"What do you know," Abraxos demanded.

"I think I killed someone. We have to find them and get help if we can," Natalia blurted desperately.

"We've got this. Brother take her home and get her cleaned up. Let us know if she remembers anything else," Abraxos told him.

"Yeah. There's no need for you guys to be here. Aison and Dante will be here soon to help," Ayil added.

Araton nodded and glanced around at the blood visible in the room. There was little doubt about what had happened, and it made him worry about Natalia. He couldn't bear to see her destroyed by this.

Wrapping her tight, he took them to his house in the Garden District before she could respond to anyone. She staggered out of his arms when they reappeared. "Warn a girl next time. I think I'm going to be sick," she complained as she braced herself on her knees.

Araton walked from his bedroom into the bathroom and turned on the light then the multiple shower heads in the large stall. When he returned to Lia, she was standing upright and glancing around the room.

"We're in my home," he said, answering her silent question. "Let's get you cleaned up."

Natalia looked down at herself and frantically clawed at her bloody clothes. Moving to her side, Araton tugged her shirt over her head and pulled her pants off fast so she couldn't get even more upset by what she looked like.

She barely noticed she was standing in front of him in a

sports bra and underwear as she hung her head. Gently, Araton lead her to the stall that was filling with steam. Araton kicked off his shoes and toed off his socks. His shorts and pants followed suit. He had his boxer briefs on the pile before he opened the door and pushed Lia under the stream.

Her shoulders shook as he gathered her in his arms. She laid her head on his chest and cried while he washed her back and arms. He didn't want to break their connection to wash her front and legs. He needed to be close to her as much as she did at the moment.

After several minutes he had to do something to stop the flow of her tears. It wrecked him to hear her so distraught. Unsure how to make her feel better, he tilted her chin up and claimed her lips in a gentle kiss.

At least that was his intention. Things got carried away the moment their mouths met. She clawed his shoulders and licked her way into his mouth. Their tongues tangled wetly, making him go from zero to sixty in the blink of an eye.

He hadn't been sexually aroused before that second, but now his desire for her burned him alive and stole all rational thought with it. He lifted the bottom of her sports bra and broke the kiss long enough to pull it over her head.

His hard cock was trapped between their hard bodies. Her green eyes looked up at him for several long seconds. He had no idea what she was searching for, as his hands clenched on her hips.

Licking her lips, she lowered her head and kissed his chest while she ran her hands up his back. He picked her up and claimed her mouth once again. Their mouths moved together while she wrapped her legs around his waist.

The change in position placed his erection against the heat of her core. She writhed and moved while he grabbed handfuls of her lush ass and squeezed. When she was breathless from his kisses, she broke away and gazed at him with lust filled eyes.

"I'm going to fuck you, Dove. Say no now if you don't want that," he informed her. He needed to be absolutely certain before he moved forward.

"Took you long enough, Wings," she replied with a sexy smile.

With a growl he lifted her higher and placed kisses on each of her breasts. She responded readily and with enthusiasm. Her moans increased as he pinched, licked and sucked on her nipples. Her legs fell away from his waist and he took advantage.

Wrapping one arm around her back, he used the other and removed her panties one inch at a time while he continued laving attention on her breasts. By the time the panties were sitting in a wet pile on the floor she was wiggling and trying to rub against him.

"Do you need something?"

"You wicked angel. I need you to rub my clit and fuck me," she informed him on a groan.

"How's this?" He asked and brought their bodies together. His move sent pleasure racing through his body. Her slick channel was fucking perfect. His shaft throbbed and his seed threatened to explode from his body in an instant.

"Yes," she hissed. "Make me forget."

Araton nearly stopped at those words, but he needed the same thing. It tore him up inside to keep seeing her devastated face and distraught sobs. He needed to replace that image with something better.

"I will fuck you until you are screaming my name. But You will remember that you aren't evil. We will beat this," he vowed to her.

Wrapping her arms around his neck, she bit down on his bottom lip and rocked her core over his cock. His mind went blank as all he could think about was not coming yet. Claiming her mouth, he took control and poured all of his desire for her into his kiss.

With one arm holding her up, he used the other to tease her opening while his shaft rubbed over her clit. She was dripping wet and eager as she tried to push into his fingers.

Araton wanted to go slow and savor the moment, but he was too far gone. He would make it up to her, he thought as he inserted one finger then added another to ensure she was ready for him.

Removing his hand, he adjusted his cock and paused with the tip at her entrance. Capturing her gaze, Araton looked at her while he drove home. That was the first thought that ran through his head when he was balls deep inside his female. Home. He'd never felt more in his life.

Grabbing her ass with both hands, he pulled out then plunged back inside. Her cry of pleasure as her head fell back on her shoulders was music to his ears. He lowered his head and kissed her nipple while he slowly fucked her.

Leaning her against the wall, Araton used his hips to keep her in place and cupped her cheeks. When she lowered her head, he pressed his mouth to hers and licked inside her mouth.

His thrusts increased in tempo with her noises and the way her body clenched and throbbed around him. His cock slid in and out of her faster and harder as he got closer to climax.

Reaching down, he rubbed her clit, making her cry out against his mouth. "Come all over me," he told her when he broke their kiss.

"God yes. Harder," she begged.

Thrusting, Araton flared his wings to give him more leverage. The move made her eyes flare wide as if she'd forgotten an angel was fucking her. The sexy minx reached up and grabbed onto his wings. The contact sizzled and it was when her small grip shifted to his wing insertions in his back that a hoarse cry left his body.

No one had ever touch him there like that and it fucking felt amazing. Growling, he pressed his mouth to hers again and plunged inside her fast and hard. He increased pressure on her clit, rubbing in fast circles.

She broke away this time to cry out his name at the moment her core clenched around him so tight he could hardly move. The short thrusts set him off and his seed exploded out of his body.

Lowering his head to her shoulder, he stood there panting with his cock still erect inside her. That took the edge off, but he wanted so much more from her. It frightened him enough to pull out and lower her to the floor.

"That was amazing. Give me a few minutes to rest and we can do that again," she told him.

He gave her a half smile then kissed her gently before turning away to wash his hair and body. "You should get some rest, Dove. You've had a long night."

That sobered her. "What's going on with me?"

"I'm taking you to meet Marie Leveau in a couple days and she will give us answers. I think you need another distraction, so you don't let this eat you up inside," he said in a husky voice as he turned back to face her.

Her gaze went to his erection. His cock jerked under the attention and he cursed himself. So much for keeping the distance between them. But he'd fuck her constantly if it meant keeping her mind off the ugly things she might have done. This urge to protect her from the evil in the world left him off kilter and adrift. One thing he knew was he hadn't yet had enough of her, so he was going to indulge while keeping her mind occupied.

*L*ia was beside herself. Araton had arrived at her door a few days ago with news that she was going to meet Marie Leveau herself. Of all the impossible things she'd discovered this was the most exciting.

As a NOLA native she was very familiar with the Queen of Voodoo and her legend. Life had been so chaotic, and she'd spent so much time trying to keep her shit together that she hadn't stopped to wonder if Marie actually existed.

The past few days seemed to have drug out for eons. She knew it was because she'd been using every ounce of energy to remain rooted in the here and now. Araton had hovered close like a man-sized bird of prey. There was no mistaking his hunger for her, but after that one night of passion he hadn't tried to be with her again.

And she hadn't pushed it. The unknown was too much for her to risk bringing harm to her angel. She'd seen what came out of Hell. There was nothing that would make her leave the world without one of its best protectors.

Araton was ready to throw caution to the wind, but she refused to give into his impulses. It took almost as much effort to make sure they were always around someone else when she wasn't patrolling.

She'd gotten to know the Dark Warriors extremely well since she spent all of her time at their manor. The Vampire King was terrifying, but she understood what made him that way.

It was more than obvious his daughter was traumatized. But then who wouldn't be given that she'd been hunted relentlessly from the moment she was conceived. Izzy was one tough girl. Lia liked her courage and determination. When she initially discovered why the Princess was in NOLA, she was surprised they wanted to put her in danger.

After getting to know her and her father better, Lia understood that neither of them could stand to place Elsie or Cian at risk with her presence. Her mom and brother meant more to Izzy than her own life. That was something she had in common with the Princess.

She hadn't been home to see her family because she wasn't entirely sure she wasn't being turned evil. Ever since they'd shot through her body, she felt an underlying presence of darkness. That was the only way she could describe the black hole of malicious energy that sat like a placid pool in her chest.

Every once in a while, that dark fluid started to froth, and waves slapped against the walls of her chest. It was those times she sought Araton out and used her connection to him to ground her in the present.

A couple times she blacked out and came to with Araton holding her near the sight of another ritual sacrifice. And because he'd been close to her, he watched her disappear. At some point they had bonded so closely with each other he was able to track her in time to stop the ritual from happening and save her.

"You ready to go meet up with the Voodoo Queen?" Araton asked as he entered her kitchen.

"More than ready. I want this thing out of me," she told him honestly as she set her plate in the sink and walked out her back door.

"Wrap your arms around me and hold on," he instructed her.

Swallowing against the desire making her lightheaded, Lia stepped close to his body and wrapped her arms around his neck. Electricity zapped her, making her shudder. It was familiar to her by now. Her angel had just turned them invisible.

His red wings extended out to his sides and he bent his knees before they took off into the air. The wind whipped her ponytail around their faces, making her bury her head in the crook of his neck. She watched the city pass beneath them for several seconds unable to say anything because she was overwhelmed by the experience, but also because she couldn't hear anything past the wind whistling loudly in her ears. All too soon they descended into a cemetery. One she hadn't been inside in nearly a decade.

Dust billowed around them when they landed. She could hear birds chirping in the distance and wind whispering like the voices of the dead as it traveled between the tombs. When their vision cleared, she let go of Araton and looked around. "Her tomb is over here," she informed him.

They walked along the narrow aisle with the long wall of tombs on one side and the larger family ones on the other. The long wall had dozens of single burial sites. Some with square openings and others with curved tops. All of them had marble slabs sealing the dead inside. Most of the structures were narrow, rectangular buildings that stood about fifteen feet tall.

Plaster covered most of them, but bricks showed through

in various places. It gave the structures an aged and worn look. Actually, everything looked like it was one windstorm away from crumbling into dust. Undoubtedly, every inch of the place carried centuries of stories, magic and energy.

Towards the back the white marble, gothic style tombs were located. Lifting her head she could see the large circular, multi-story tomb that was for Italian residents long ago.

They traveled through the maze of tombs and reached one that looked better cared for than most in the place. New plaster covered the bricks and the pristine plaque on the side carried her name while the top of three marble slabs sealing the front was etched with her name.

"How do we get inside?" She asked. She cocked her head to the side and looked at Araton when he remained silent.

"I didn't take her for a pink person," he murmured as if he was lost in thought.

"The city painted it after it was vandalized. It used to be brighter. It's barely noticeable now," she replied.

Shaking his head, he approached the front. "She never gave me instructions…" His voice trailed away as the three layers of marble slabs shifted inward as if they were a door.

Glancing back at her, Araton instructed her to stay behind him. Nodding, she followed him into the dark interior. There was a moment where she hesitated on the threshold. "I don't know if I can go inside. You're walking through the remains of her ancestors. That's highly disrespectful."

Pausing, Araton glared back at her. "There are no coffins here."

"We bury our dead differently. The bodies are placed on platforms in the tomb for a year and a day after death. After that time has passed the staff remove the cover and brush what remains to the back where it falls to accumulate on the ground. Right where you are walking," she informed him.

"I appreciate da concern, Natalia," a woman's voice said in

a thick Cajun accent. The words seemed to come from nowhere and everywhere. They were accompanied by a power that washed over her with full-body tingles. "I have taken steps ta protect my dead."

Lia stared wide-eyed at Araton who returned to her side and grabbed her hand. He tugged her through, and they walked for a couple seconds down a narrow dirt path. The same brick walls lined the sides, but the air wasn't musty like she anticipated.

Instead, an earthy vibrant scent permeated the area. Within a few seconds the path ended, and they stepped into a large room. It was obviously underground given the water dripping from one of the corners.

The roof and walls were stained wood slats. It almost felt like they were inside a coffin which was ridiculous. The furnishings were high-end antiques. There was a brocade chair that looked like something from the Victorian era. So did the Persian rug. Both were shades of burgundy, but Lia couldn't pull her gaze from the stunning woman sitting in the chair like a Queen.

Like most from her era Marie wore tignon of vibrant gold and an elaborate headdress. There were gems of all kinds. Rubies, sapphires, emeralds, and diamonds. Lia imagined her hair was black but couldn't see for sure because it was all tucked away and hidden.

She had creamy café-au-lait skin that glowed in the candlelight illuminating the room. Candelabras lay on side tables near the woman, highlighting the luxurious gold and red shawl around her shoulders.

"Thank you for helping me," Natalia said as she crossed to the woman.

Marie stood up and her floor length skirts swished across the floor. "Your angel would have it no other way. He went ta great lengths ta help you." Lia was astonished while not being surprised at all by the news. She was falling for the sexy angel. But was he falling for her, too?

* * *

ARATON HID the reactions tearing through his mind. It wasn't easy to hide the maelstrom raging inside. He'd grown more and more attached to Natalia as the days passed. He'd never understood his brother and sister for wanting to mate with another and tie their lives inexplicably to someone else.

Since meeting Lia, he understood so much better. The human had come to mean so much to him. And only part of it was his desire to explore her body. She was brave and faced challenges head on while putting others before herself. That selflessness was extremely rare in any beings. Few angels could say the same as this woman.

Now as he watched emotions pass over Lia's face when Marie told her what Araton had done to ensure her survival and protection, he wanted to pull her into his arms and kiss her senseless.

Instead, he banked his desire and turned to the Voodoo Queen. "Can you tell if she is possessed by a demon?" Next to him Lia tensed and moved away from his body. He didn't like the distance and closed it immediately. He refused to allow her to pull away now. She hadn't asked him to leave yet. He wasn't going to let her entertain anything of the sort now.

Marie glided closer to them and withdrew a vial from her pocket. Pouring something into her hand, the Queen of Voodoo blew shimmery powder in her face. Natalia stiffened and started falling to the floor. He caught her before she hit the ground.

As he watched her eyes rolled back in her head and she started convulsing. Shadows swirled from her chest. The second they touched him they burned him. Unable to keep hold of her, Araton lost his hold on Natalia.

His body shook from the thousand needles stabbing into him at once and watched as she hit the floor. Marie stood near and chanted something in another language. His female arched and cried out even more. Marie must be forcing the demons out.

Araton waited and watched cursing his helplessness as Lia writhed and moaned. The shadows never left Lia's body entirely though. "What's wrong? Why aren't they leaving her?"

Marie waved her arms and mist seeped from her to enclose Lia. She stopped the agonized cries and her body stilled. Marie turned a somber gaze to Araton. "She is no' possessed. Dis is much more complicated dan dat."

Unable to resist any longer, Araton hurried and scooped Lia into his arms. She immediately burrowed into the hollow at his throat. "What do you mean?" He demanded. His eyes never left Natalia's face. She no longer looked like she was suffering, but she was paler than before.

"I mean your human is an open portal to da Underworld," Marie explained with a somber expression.

"What?" Lia cried out. Araton glanced down and saw that all the color had drained from Natalia's face. She looked closer to a corpse than anything alive. "Demons get in because I acted as a doorway for them? That would mean those people are dead because of me."

Marie ran her hand over Lia's cheek. Araton set her on her feet and wrapped an arm around her waist. No matter what they discovered he would never forsake Natalia. He poured everything he was feeling for her into his touch.

"Demons can get in through you, but what I sense is you were infected with a spell that will be powerful enough to allow Lucifer's possession. At least for a limited time."

Natalia cried out in denial and her body seemed to crumple beside Araton. Keeping her close, he met Marie's steady stare. "Explain. We have heard Lucifer is on Earth possessing another but haven't confirmed that. I have been with her constantly and not sensed demons passing through her, let alone Lucifer."

"You misunderstand. Lucifer will use her body. Because she is tethered ta Hell he can open da connection and take over, using her ta wreak havoc on Earth. Only demons of his caliber can utilize such a portal. It bypasses the binds keeping him in da Underworld."

Lia opened and closed her mouth several times, but nothing came out of her mouth. "Okay, so she is the connection that allows Lucifer to take action on Earth. How do we rid her of it?" Araton cut in. He was trying to allow her time to process and ask questions, but that was the only issue that really mattered.

He refused to allow Lia to think of what Lucifer could have done while inhabiting her body the night she woke up in the bayou covered in blood. Sure, there had been dead animals nearby, but he had suspected then and even more so now that more had gone on that night that she wasn't aware of.

"Da only way you can eliminate dis connection is ta create one of Light dat is far stronger and will override da one wit Lucifer," Marie explained as she walked back to her chair.

"You mean create a connection to Heaven?" Natalia asked.

"Dat is precisely what I mean," The Queen of Voodoo told her with a smile.

"Okay. That's good. I already believe in God and go to church as often as possible. I'm friends with you guys. I can go pray more. I even bet Pastor Quince will give me a blessing."

Marie was back on her feet and walking back to them. "Dat is not enough. It must be an intimate connection. A permanent and unbreakable one dat changes who you are on a fundamental level. Only dat will ensure you cannot be used by Lucifer."

Araton understood precisely what the Queen of Voodoo meant and knew the moment Lia understood, as well. He couldn't process what she seemed to be experiencing as he ran through the implications himself.

He was falling for the stunning human, but he wasn't ready to mate with her. Unfortunately, from what Marie was saying he, or another angel had to mate with her to destroy the link that had been forced on her by Lucifer's demons.

Not moving forward with mating Lia and forcing the change in her DNA would leave the entire world at risk. Especially, Natalia. She would never survive it she was forced to perform the acts Lucifer wanted.

Eventually Lia would become accustomed to being taken over and remain awake to witness what he forced her to do. That would destroy everything that made her the most compassionate, courageous and determined woman he'd ever met.

"I think I understand. You're saying I need to marry an angel or something," Natalia replied then tilted her head to look at Araton.

"Not exactly. Mating is far more intense than marriage. When supernaturals mate it's for life and no force in any realm can break that bond," Araton explained.

"Mate…like Izzy's parents, Zander and Elsie. They're Fated Mates, right?" Lia clarified.

"Dat is precisely what I mean. Some have Fated Mates. Angels and several others select who they bind their lives to and much like other supernaturals doing so with a human alters the human's cellular structure, so they live as long as their mate. Dat change is what will eliminate your bond to da Underworld and Lucifer."

Lia's face crumpled as Marie explained more. Araton didn't understand why each of the Voodoo Queen's words landed on Natalia like blows. "I always knew I was destined for greatness, I just never realized it would be because I sacrificed myself to save the world."

That explained it. "No fucking way. That will not happen. We don't have time to get into it more right now. We have a house to clear of trapped ghosts and demonic energy," Araton barked.

"Thank you for helping me, Mrs. Leveau. I don't know how I can repay you."

"Your angel has already rendered payment." Marie waved her arm, causing her many bangles to jingle as she moved. The world went black the next second then blindingly bright.

Araton blinked as the midday sun was high overhead. When the spots cleared, he noticed he was standing in the cemetery next to Lia. "Hold on, Dove. We have a house to deal with."

"Just promise me one thing. You will never let me become Lucifer's pawn again. You have to kill me before that happens," she said as she wrapped her arms around his neck.

He tugged her close while his entire body protested the request she made. The world needed her in it. He didn't think he could harm one hair on her head. That left him one choice. And he didn't know how he felt about that. Kill her or mate her? There was no going back if he chose the latter.

Giving into the desire running rampant through his body, he lowered his head and took her mouth in a kiss hot enough to melt their clothes. He devoured her and couldn't temper his mouth one bit. He couldn't get enough of her.

It was rare that he recalled a female after he had sex with

her. Not because he didn't care, but because his mission always took precedence. It was dangerous for him to lose sight of the fact that he and his fellow Warrior Angels (along with a handful of supernatural Dark Warriors) were all that stood between innocents and hordes of demons.

And, yet here he was standing in the middle of a cemetery kissing the life out of a human that acted as a conduit of sorts for Lucifer. While there was so many more important things he needed to deal with. The most important of which was a house that had so many layers of demonic energy and trapped spirits in it, he'd been forced to go to the Queen of Voodoo for help.

Despite everything weighing on him, there was no way he could stop from grabbing hold of Lia's plush ass. He tried to pour how much he needed and wanted her to be free of this burden into his kiss. Problem was, he wasn't so sure he could do what it took to save her and mate the female.

CHAPTER 15

*A*raton was panting and more determined than ever to make sure Natalia survived this with her goodness intact when he broke away from Lia's mouth. Her pupils were dilated, her lips red and swollen and her breathing was uneven as she gazed up at him.

He felt like he hung the moon at that moment. To make her come undone like that regardless of their current situation meant she not only wanted him, but trusted him as well. It meant more to him than he ever thought possible to have earned her trust.

He adjusted his erection in his pants and glared up at the sky. It was late afternoon and they had more shit to deal with. "We will be picking up where we left off, Wings."

That startled him and his gaze lowered back to hers. "You think so?"

"I know so," she said as she cupped him through the fabric of his jeans. "I'm done waiting for you to approach me again. I'm not evil. I've become Lucifer's bitch and I am going to experience the best sex of my life at least one more time before I die."

Araton closed the gap between them and his face was mere inches from hers. "You. Will. Not. Be. Dying," he bit out through clenched teeth. "Now. Hold on. We really are leaving this time."

Her soft hands traveled over his shoulders and wrapped around the back of his neck. "My Fate is out of my hands now. There is no way I am going to force some rando angel to mate with me just to save my life."

Araton exploded off the ground with her clutched to his torso. She yelped in his ear and shook in his hold. He knew he'd frightened her, but he couldn't regain control of his temper. And he couldn't promise to be the one to mate her. He still didn't know if he wanted to tie his life to hers forever. It was a long damn time.

Landing a few seconds later, Araton still wasn't any calmer. But he did manage to shift his focus to the next crisis on his to do list. He was so fucking ready to blow this damn house up. It was at the center of every problem in his life at the moment. The massive grey home sat seemingly innocuous on the corner. If you didn't have the ability to sense demonic energy that is.

"Are your brothers here?" Lia asked, avoiding their previous conversation as well.

"Yeah they should be inside," he replied and headed for the front door. The streets were mostly empty with a couple cars heading away from their location.

Demonic energy nearly tossed him on his ass the second he opened the door. "Abraxos, Ayil," he called out.

"Here, brother." The call came from the room where he first discovered Natalia. They entered and he nodded at the two males that had always been at his side. He suddenly wanted to ask them what he should do about Lia, but now wasn't the time.

They were sprinkling the substance Marie Leveau gave

them around the room. Araton quickly joined them and did the same. They had finished downstairs and were about to head up to the next level when blood started dripping down the walls.

"What's happening?" Natalia called out.

"They're trying to stop the ritual," Araton told her.

"They won't show up, will they?" She asked as she bit her lower lip.

"Not likely. The sun weakens them to the point even humans would stand a chance against them," he explained. The sound of moans and shouts echoed throughout the house. The volume was quiet at the moment. They'd just begun to stir the ghosts trapped there.

"Thank God," she said, and he noticed her shoulders lower as the tension left them. Some of the tension reappeared a few seconds later when the pale outline of a man appeared in the middle of the long wood table. His image hovered there for a second then darted toward the ceiling. Several more people appeared as Araton checked his work.

Araton went back to work, wanting to remove this from Lucifer's arsenal. The demonic energy intensified as they stirred shit up while they worked. Araton had to focus on the house itself to remind himself why they weren't burning it to the ground.

They all moved up the stairs to repeat the process there. The house was old but had been restored and cared for in the intervening years. The scars and dents in the flooring and walls told a story all their own. You'd never know on first glance that the story was really a nightmare.

The furniture was modern with antique pieces sprinkled throughout. Decorations hung on the walls. Some were palm leaves. Others were of the architecture in the Quarter. And then there was the wood signs proclaiming that all were welcome. The wood floors were stained a dark color while the walls were pale grey. Until the blood started pouring down them. Then you got a much clearer picture of the house's story.

Araton's favorite room in the house had to be the kitchen. The appliances were all stainless steel and the countertops were marble. It was the position in the house that let in the afternoon light that made it so appealing. The light cast out the shadows that seemed to linger in every other room.

Araton glanced out the window when he was treating a living room and saw Aison in the courtyard keeping watch. He knew Micah was in the streets in front of the house doing the same. They didn't expect trouble, but he and his brothers were accustomed to including the Dark Warriors when possible for an extra layer of protection for humans.

"I'm calling in the others to help the spirits cross over," Ayil called out as he stuck his head in the room.

"Sounds good," Araton replied then smiled with Ayil when they heard their brother.

"My heads spinnin' round and round. But in the seasons of wither. We'll stand and deliver. Be strong and laugh and Shout, shout, shout at the Devil," Abraxos crooned as he worked from another part of the house.

"He sings a lot, doesn't he?" Lia interjected. She'd been following Araton quietly and watching as they worked. She'd been around them long enough to pick up on one of Abraxos's quirks.

"That he does. Let's head up to the attic. I hear the other angels arriving downstairs to help the deceased cross over," Araton informed her. "We can send the ghosts back down to them."

Nodding, she followed behind him up the narrow staircase. When they reached the attic, Araton fought hard to hold back his reaction. There were countless ghosts crammed in the area.

Some images were of people in cages. They'd clearly been tortured. Hands were missing from one young man. Another held a woman that was missing her eyes. And still more had their throats slit.

One guy had been decapitated. Another had a bull's head sewn onto his body. The sight was depraved. Beside him Lia shook. Araton couldn't even meet her gaze. They had to work fast, or they would never be able to free these poor souls. He opened his jar and began sprinkling the mixture that incited the souls around.

The walls immediately started bleeding. Araton reached the far corner and his gag reflex was doing pushups in his throat. Several babies lay there in a pile with their mothers reaching through the bars of a cage.

"Don't come over here," he told Lia as he sprinkled his concoction around the wood floor. He'd moved a few feet when he realized she never responded to him. He turned to reassure her that they were offering these people peace.

His blood froze in his veins when he didn't see her anywhere. There was no doubt she couldn't handle the images in that room. Araton had to force himself to finish the attic before he went in search of Natalia.

He ran into Abraxos on the second floor. "Have you seen Lia?"

His brother glanced around and shook his head. "Not for a bit. Did you get the attic?"

"Yeah. That was worse than the seventh circle in Hell. So many lost their lives in there. It's what sent Lia away," Araton explained. "I'd better find her and make sure she's okay."

"You've got it bad, little brother," Abraxos teased.

"Fuck off," he snapped and headed down the hall. A rapid search of the rooms on the second floor told him she wasn't there.

By the time he reached the lower level he was certain she

had to be outside. With the angels working to help the spirits on the first floor, she wouldn't have hung around. She still wasn't comfortable around anyone but him.

He walked through the kitchen and froze on the back porch as he looked into the courtyard. "What the fuck?" He growled. Denial put up blocks in his mind. That could not be her.

Natalia lifted her head and stared at him. Her familiar green eyes were nowhere to be seen. Instead vibrant red looked back at him. The creature before him had her long silky black hair tied into a ponytail. And her round face. Its upper lip was even smaller than the lower exactly like Lia's.

The smile that curved the thing's mouth was not even remotely like the woman he was falling in love with. A glint of light shone in his eyes when she stood up. The light reflected off the bloody knife she held clutched in her hand.

"Abraxos, Ayil," he screamed and lunged into action.

"You're too late to save your friend, Warrior," Lia replied in a deep, malevolent voice that was nothing like hers. "And you will lose this one, too." Lucifer in Lia's body pointed to Aison where he lay in a puddle of blood.

His right arm looked like it had been cut from his body and there was a hole in his chest. Lucifer was dissecting him in broad daylight. Araton collided with Lia's and had to ignore the fact that he took her down with enough force to crack her skull.

Lucifer was fast and swiped the blade in his hand across Araton's shoulder. Growling, he tried to grab hold of Lia's arm and stop her from hurting him. He was reluctant to really harm her.

That hesitance cost him when Lucifer managed to bite down on the top of his wing. She tore out a chunk of his flesh. Bringing his legs up, he kicked her off of his chest. She growled and flew back toward him. Her knife cut a slash down his arm before he managed to grab hold of her hand.

She bucked and kicked and tried to pull her hand from his grip. He squeezed hard enough he heard bones snap and felt them grind together. Regret tasted bitter on his tongue, but rage overpowered all of that.

"You will not take this woman from me," he informed Lucifer.

"I already have," Lucifer cackled. "There is no magic capable of destroying my connection to her."

He wanted to curse because Marie had told him the same thing. The only way he could save Lia was to mate her and create a bond that overpowered the one Lucifer had forced on her.

"I haven't had so much fun in thousands of years," Lucifer continued. "Humans make the best sounds when I eviscerate them. I can't wait to go beyond blood play with this one."

Abraxos and Ayil came running out the back door and halted halfway between them and Aison. "Help Aison. You need to call Jace right away so he can save the arm," Araton told them.

They looked torn for a split second then Abraxos had his phone in hand while Ayil rushed to the injured Dark Warrior. Natalia was going to take matters into her own hands when she learned she had nearly killed someone she considered a friend.

Araton couldn't think about that much more or he wouldn't be able to help her banish the devil from her body. He called his sword of Light to his hand. "I will not allow you to kill anyone else while in her body," Araton informed him.

He forced all soft emotions he had for Lia to a separate part of his mind and allowed his anger and hatred for Lucifer to surface. At the same time, he cast a shield around the area that would hopefully prevent Lucifer from teleporting. It was unclear how it would work on Lia, but it was able to stop archdemons from getting away.

"You are an abomination that will never truly be free from Hell," Araton told the devil. Lucifer looked around for a couple seconds then snarled at Araton and took off in the opposite direction. Araton took to the air and landed in front of him.

He had to lunge and catch Lia when her eyes rolled back in her head and her body started convulsing. Jace ran by him and headed toward Aison while Ayil came to his side.

"What happened?"

"Lucifer took over her body. Marie told us today that Lia is a conduit for the King of Hell. That's what has been happening to her. Lucifer hijacks her body and takes over. He attacked Aison."

"Fuck," Ayil cursed as he knelt next to them. "We can't let her walk freely knowing Lucifer can take the wheel. Did Marie give you a way to banish his connection?"

Araton lowered his head to the top of Lia's. There was only one way to save her. Nodding, he looked up at his brother. "I have to mate her and establish a more powerful bond with Heaven. Nothing else will sever the connection. And, I don't know if I can do that."

Ayil cursed under his breath and watched the activity while Jace worked on healing Aison. Dante and Micah had shown up at some point, too. Abraxos was in the thick of it with the healer and unaware of the conversation between them.

Meeting his gaze again, Ayil ran a hand through his hair. "Mating is blessing of the highest caliber. I would never change binding myself to Kennex. She is my everything. But if you don't love this woman and feel like you cannot take another breath without her then you shouldn't mate her."

"How can you say that? It would be saving her life."

Araton was torn by this very fact. And needed to make sure he was thinking straight. Something that seemed impossible when Lia was around.

"Yes, it would save her life, but to be tied to someone you do not love will make it impossible for you to fulfill your duty. Something inside would die with the forced bond. It will turn sour and rot you away from the inside," Ayil replied with a grin face.

"I can't kill her. And if anyone else tries I'm fairly certain I will stand in their way. I'm…falling for her. I'm not sure exactly what I feel about her, but it's killing me to even think about her being injured or worse," Araton admitted.

"Then it looks like you have some thinking to do. In the meantime, take her to Heaven. See if having her there will buy you some time to figure shit out. These times she is blacking out are taking a toll on her emotionally. I get the sense she won't tolerate knowing she is a risk to others very well," Ayil said as he stood and brushed off his pants.

"Thank you for not insisting she's either killed or mated right now. Let me know how Aison does. I need to get her away from here," Araton told his brother as he stood and cradled Lia close to his chest.

"Will do," Ayil promised. Araton placed a kiss to Lia's lips then teleported them to his house in the Garden District. What the fuck was he going to do about this mess? He couldn't deny that he cared for her, but mating was an entirely different matter.

CHAPTER 16

"What the fuck are they doing?" Slate murmured with a scowl as they hid behind several parked vehicles.

None of it made sense to Dante. Archdemons and their skirm didn't set up shop inside a sports stadium. Why were they taking such a major chance with this? It didn't make any sense.

They were getting cocky for sure and it made him uneasy. Discovering Lucifer could hijack Natalia's body was a sobering thought. She might be a human female, but the Lord of the Underworld used her body to a chilling degree.

He had nearly cut Aison to shreds. Jace had been able to save his life and his arm. Araton had come out of the house before he cut Aison's heart from his chest. An immortal could survive the injury, but it would have been a long and arduous healing process.

Thanks to the fast thinking of Araton and his brothers, Aison was making a rapid recovery and would be back on his feet in a few days. Dante couldn't stop wondering what would have happened if Jace hadn't been home along with Gerrick to open a portal to the LaLaurie Mansion.

Abraxos had FaceTimed the healer in order to give him the visual he would need to open a portal to the location. Aison was back at Les Augres before Dante had heard what went down.

There was little doubt in his mind that the demons were taking more risk because they were certain Lucifer was going to win. It was the only thing that made sense. After thousands upon thousands of years frozen in a lake in Hell Lucifer was moving freely in the Underworld and now able to cross to Earth in the body of a human woman.

"I'd say they're moving in," Dante replied as he kept scanning the front entrance.

"We need to take these fuckers out. This stadium might be useless to humans at the moment, but the Saints will be back," Micah snarled in a low voice.

"But where is the archdemon? There's always one close by to control their minions and the lower demons. Those hellhounds tend to get bitey when their aggression isn't directed," Luke added.

"We've counted eleven so far. Let's engage now before more arrive. We can see what the setup is inside the stadium," Dante ordered them. "I'll text Ayil and Abraxos. Araton is remaining with Natalia to ensure Lucy doesn't take the wheel again."

Pulling his phone from his back pocket, Dante fired off a text to the two brothers as well as Zander filling them in on what they'd discovered. He'd barely shoved his cell back inside his pocket when growling made the hair on his arms stand on end.

Spinning around, Dante came face to snout with a massive hellhound. Fucking thing smelled like death. Teeth snapped at him making him jump back. Awkwardly, he tried to reach his sheathed *sgian dubh* while he was in motion.

Unfortunately, he'd only recently been training full-time and he landed on his elbow. The crack echoed around him followed by excruciating pain several seconds later. The demon dog clamped its jaws around Dante's thigh.

Finally extricating his weapons from under his armpits, Dante stabbed out at the beast's head. The knife sunk into the hound's skull, making it yelp. With a growl, it let go of Dante's leg and swiped at him with one big paw.

It wasn't until Dante climbed to his feet that he realized the others were engaged in battles of their own. Dante's blade was still sticking out of the hound's head, so he grabbed it and twisted while he plunged the other into one of its eyes.

A pus demon came at him from behind and grabbed him around the waist. His hand sank into soft, slimy flesh as he shoved one of his hands behind him. Pulling the knife free from the gelatinous beast, Dante jumped as much as his injured leg would allow and stabbed both weapons through the pus demon's skull.

He launched off its falling body and into a skirm. The rapid-fire thrusts managed to ash the fucker after his third strike. Two hellhounds approach him from different angles. Dante jumped onto the hood of a car and kicked one of them in the head.

He was flying through the air toward the other creature before the first got its bearings. Roaring out his frustration, Dante's blade sank into the top of the hound's skull. The one he kicked had recovered from the blow and was leaping over the vehicle toward Dante.

Taking a running start, Dante slid on his injured leg and nearly passed out from the pain. He hadn't thought that through. It took great effort to force himself to lift his hand and eviscerate the demon dog as he traveled under its body.

Jumping to his feet, he almost toppled when a fist slammed into the side of his head. Dante punched a fist toward the rage demon and tried to keep a lid on his anger. It would only fuel this enemy.

Instead he relished the feel of flesh bruising under his blows. When the rage demon staggered, Dante sliced a blade across its throat. Black blood spurted out of the injury. The specks that landed on his exposed skin burned. The rage demon managed to inflict another blow as it went down.

At first Dante didn't realize what had happened, but then the warm liquid gushed down the side of his neck telling him the creature's claws managed to inflict a deep wound.

Slate was at his side, panting a second later. The Dark Warrior placed a hand over the wound and applied pressure. "The bleeding isn't stopping. Do you need me to take you back to the manor?"

Dante knew why it wasn't stopping. He hadn't fed properly for months. The little sips he'd gotten from kisses and caresses weren't enough to feed his inner demon. Dante was going to have to make the time and find a female today or he would be down for longer than he could afford.

Being back in the thick of the action was what kept him going. Ever since returning from the Underworld with Rhys and Kellen he'd been searching for something to fulfill him. He wished every day that his friend Nikko was still with them, but he loved his new role. It gave him a purpose he'd been needing for centuries.

Cambions were creatures of heat, fun and passion, but that had become common place for Dante over the centuries. His role in the Alliance had been minimal until recently when he discovered new fun for him.

Feeling light-headed, Dante nearly opened his mouth to say yes, he wanted to go back to the manor. His need to see this through kept his mouth shut. "Fucker got me good. I'll be fine soon enough. The bleeding has already slowed." At least that last part was the truth. The bleeding had slowed but hadn't stopped.

Glancing around the lot, he noticed the bodies littering the asphalt like a macabre art display. It was incredibly satisfying to see so many dead demons in one place. The cars were worse for the wear which made him feel bad.

It was as he was assessing the damage to the vehicles that he realized there were far too many with the humans not venturing near the stadium at the time. "What are all these cars from? Have demons learned to drive?"

None of it made any sense. Having a pus demon behind the wheel of a car, or even a Behemoth demon, was ridiculous and made him want to laugh. Unless humans were lured to the stadium and the demons were filling it with enough sacrifices to make Lucifer strong enough to break free of the spells and cross fully to Earth in his body.

"The rental car companies don't have anywhere to park their vehicles, so they've used locations like this where they can store them while they aren't being rented," Luke explained.

"Thank the Goddess. For a minute there I was worried the demons were luring humans here for one massive sacrifice," Dante admitted. "That would be a fucking disaster since I'm fairly certain it would generate enough power for Lucifer to get free of Hell."

"Don't even think it," Micah hissed under his breath as if the demons might like the idea and go for it.

"Let's sneak in there and see what we can discover," Dante instructed as he limped toward the entrance while holding a hand over his wounded neck.

"This entire place smells like a dead rat's asshole," Slate complained as they snuck through the gate.

Dante winced as a loud creak echoed throughout the area. "We need to get through the entrance and head to the field through an upper passage. Demons tend to head down more often than up."

The warriors nodded their heads and followed him through the empty place. Dante lightened his steps so that they didn't echo like thunder through the halls. Dante had never been inside the stadium for a game and wondered at the layout.

There were shuttered vendor booths along the inner curve with stairwells interspersed between where he imagined people would buy food and drinks. Along the outer curve he saw some bathrooms and lots of windows.

Everything was white. Or some shade of it. The walls and the flooring were so similar they blended into one bland shade. Even the silver of the panels for the locations where products were sold blended into the whole.

The dark openings for the stairs were the only things that broke up the view. Increasing his steps, he lifted his hand and left his neck injury when only a trickle of blood still seeped from the ragged edged wound.

Dante climbed some steps and headed up into the chairs that filled the circumference of the place. He swore there had to be at least seventy thousand seats. If they even filled a quarter of the place with sacrifices, then they would have no problem generating enough energy to free Lucifer.

The thought made him sick to his stomach. Every living thing on the planet would be at risk if the demons managed that. There were times in life when something occurred to renew one's dedication to a cause or reaffirm the reason for living.

This was one of those moments for Dante. He would do

everything in his power to keep Lucifer from crossing over. He might not have much in his life, but most of his closest friends has discovered their Fated Mates in recent years and were starting to have babies.

The love and new life inspired Dante to want to do his part. And in the back of his mind he realized he might have a Fated Mate out there somewhere. Not that he believed he would be blessed with one.

He'd done too many awful things to have earned that privilege. Perhaps if he'd come to his senses and fled from the Underworld sooner, but not now. Focusing on what he could actually do something about, he ducked between two rows of chairs and trained his gaze on the green field below.

The lighting in the place was awful. Out in the halls the windows allowed the moonlight to fill the area and make it easier to see what was around them. In the middle of the stadium the lighting was horrendous. He could see because his vision was better than a human's, but small details were impossible to pick out.

The one thing that was obvious was the grass below them, filling most of the area. The stuff filled a flat area of about two hundred square feet below them. There were also numbered white lines at regular intervals on the field. He thought the marks were used in some of the human sports. Zander and some of the warriors in Seattle loved watching football and baseball and he recalled them talking about it. But Dante had never been interested, so he retained little of the information.

The most important details were the creatures crawling all over the place. There were far fewer demons on the grass than he expected. Maybe twenty-five or thirty. And, they seemed to be setting up homes for themselves. There were about eight or nine hellhounds circling each other off to the far left on the field. Their growls filled the air right before they lunged at each other.

Dante grimaced as the beasts tore at each other. Chunks of flesh went flying through the air in black bloody masses. Pus demons stopped what they were doing and watched for several seconds before they raced over to take what looked like fabric from the area.

The demon dogs broke away from one another and attacked the pus demons. So many other types of demons were on the field with them, but none in as high of numbers as the hellhounds.

Dante noticed some skirm setting up beds on the opposite side of the field from the hounds and pus demons. This must be where they are living at the moment. Glancing at Slate, Dante whispered, "Look for the archdemon. Shit will remain chaotic if one isn't here. We can let them kill each other while we get back-up."

Slate nodded and they continued scanning the arena. The smell of brimstone and sulfur thickened as the seconds passed. There was no sign of anyone in charge. Dante tapped Slate's shoulder and nodded to the exit.

The warriors got up one at a time and headed to the stairs in a crouch. They'd almost made it to the bottom when they heard voices. Luke was in the lead and paused when he heard the noise then plastered himself to the wall.

"Where is Quinah? Someone attacked in the parking lot and we lost some," said a male voice.

"He told me to move my shit here, but hasn't been around to give me more instructions," said another.

"We are to wait here for him to show up. He was looking for Lucifer who is supposed to take over the human cop again tonight," a female told them.

It was still jarring to hear a female skirm. Archdemons had never before turned women. Dante thought it was because the female mind was so much stronger than a male's. But that was just conjecture. He wondered what brought about the change. He suspected it had to do with Lucifer gaining more of his power after he was released from being frozen in Lake Cocytus.

"I hope he gets here soon. I hate having to control the hell hounds. I can hear them fighting already," replied one of the males.

"He will get here after he finds the Dark Lord. The time of demons is nearly here. Soon enough our efforts will come to fruition. I for one want to be on Lucifer's good side when he crosses to Earth. If I'm lucky his Queen will want me as part of her personal guard," the female interjected.

"I still don't understand why he went from having us hunt for the Princess to ensuring she lives," one of the male's replied.

Dante's head snapped to meet Micah's gaze as she stood next to him. *"What the fuck?"* The Dark Warrior mouthed. Dante shook his head. There was no telling what prompted that change, but Zander wasn't going to like hearing the Dark Lord had plans for his daughter.

The Gods and Goddesses needed to leave the poor girl alone. Her entire life had been one danger after another. She'd been kidnapped by an archdemon and taken to Hell and gone through some kind of trauma when she was in Khoth.

Dante wanted to slay every archdemon on the planet then plant bombs in the Underworld to protect her from being used by any more powerful beings. Izzy deserved to have a happy carefree life.

The skirm's conversation died down. They waited several more seconds to make sure the coast was clear before they hurried down the rest of the steps and headed out of the stadium.

That little excursion left him with more questions than it answered. Dante moved as fast as his leg would allow before he pulled his phone from his back pocket and dialed Zander.

"We need to talk, Z. And, you're going to want to grab a drink for this one," Dante told one of his best friends. Dante questioned his sanity for one silent second. He wanted more purpose in life and welcomed the new assignment. Having to tell a father the devil wanted to claim his daughter never crossed his mind.

Fucking demons. Fucking up everything and causing chaos wherever they went. And, fuck the Lord of the Underworld and his desire to destroy one of the purest souls he'd ever met. Not happening on his watch.

CHAPTER 17

*A*raton brushed the hair from Lia's forehead and gazed into her peaceful face. Looking at her with her eyes closed and the lines around her eyes and mouth gone, he couldn't tell the turmoil that coursed through the sexy cop. All he saw was a beautiful woman with a spine of steel and a selflessness he rarely saw in any creature.

She stretched her arms over her head and arched her back. "Good morning," she said in a husky, sleepy voice. Of course, it shot through him and made him hard as stone.

"Afternoon," he replied, hoping she didn't recall or ask questions about what happened the day before. He didn't want the smile to vanish. Everything seemed better when she smiled at him.

"When did we get to your place? The last thing I recall was the attic in the LaLaurie….oh shit," she sat up and the green blanket fell to her lap. The sight of his shirt falling over her pert breasts distracted him for a split second.

He had changed her into one of his t-shirts after he'd gotten her to his house. Her shirt was covered in Aison's blood. No way did he want her waking up again stained with the crimson fluid. If the moment wasn't so dire, he would take a moment to appreciate how much he liked seeing her in his clothes.

"Yes, Lucifer took over, but I managed to stop him before he killed Aison," he informed her.

"Aison? He's alive?"

Nodding, Araton didn't fight the urge to offer her physical reassurances. "He's alive and will heal in no time."

"Oh God. I can't take this. I need to do something before I really hurt someone. I couldn't live with that," she whispered with a lowered head. She looked completely torn apart. He knew exactly what she was saying but he refused to lose her.

And it wasn't only because he was falling for her. The world needed her in it. She protected her kind and made life better for anyone she came in contact with. He had a plan that his brothers were helping him with, but he needed to take her to Heaven first.

"Don't say that. I am not leaving your side until we banish Lucifer for good. I'm not ready to mate you yet, but I want to take you to Heaven. I think if you spend some time there it will give us enough time to develop a relationship," he explained to her.

"I don't know. You know I will never ask you to mate me to save my life. It seems like it will be a major risk to have me there. Is it alright with Gabriel that you bring me to uh...Heaven?"

"I haven't asked Gabriel, but if Ayil was able to take his Phoenix there when she was actively plotting to blow up angels you should be welcomed with a red carpet. I mean, you're like the epitome of everything angels stand for."

Lia snorted and shook her head. "Yeah if you ignore the fact that Lucifer can supplant my consciousness anytime and he was banished from Heaven thousands of years ago after he rebelled against God and started a war that divided Heaven."

Araton laughed. It was the first moment of levity he truly felt since his sister had been kidnapped over a century ago. "You're worth the risk. And, for the record, I don't think Gabriel will mind. You're more of a warrior than those that have been trained for the position. Now, get dressed, Dove. We have a date to keep."

Climbing to her feet she headed for the bathroom. "I hope you have some better clothes for me. I don't want to go up there in just a t-shirt."

"There's an outfit in the bathroom," he told her with a smile. It took all of his effort to wait for her in his bedroom. The sound of the water running had him thinking about her standing there naked as she soaped up her body to wash it clean.

Araton's cock throbbed and his body ached. He knew how good it felt to sink into her hot, wet core and he wanted more of her. Never before had anyone consumed so much of his attention and desire.

For the first time he struggled to think of anything besides Natalia. He'd been so consumed he had asked his brothers to go to his home in Heaven and create a romantic scene for her. He and Abraxos had done it for Ayil and now they were helping him.

He hoped that by making love to her surrounded by the origin of Light energy it would infuse her with an ability to keep Lucifer in check. It wasn't that he was fighting his attraction to Lia. He had considered mating her regardless of anything else.

He would never regret forming the bond with her. And, he would mate her before she hurt herself or worse. She might not choose him in the long run, but every cell in his body said she had to survive this. That the balance of good versus evil depended on it.

"I'm ready to wow Heaven," she announced as she came out of the bathroom a few minutes later. Her long black hair hung down her back. The strands were still wet and made the locks shine in the late afternoon light streaming through his windows.

Ayil's mate Kennex had brought the soft grey top and skinny jeans for Lia. They hugged her curves like a glove. She wore no makeup and didn't need any. Her green eyes danced with amusement as she looked at him.

"You look stunning," he told her honestly.

Waving her hand, she made a pfft sound. "I can't believe this is my life now. I'm falling for a sexy Warrior Angel who has given me the best orgasms of my entire life. Other than having mind-blowing sex, I was tortured by demons and possessed by Lucifer. Now I'm being taken to Heaven. Oh, and I've met real live vampires, shifters and sorcerers."

Stepping close to her and pressing his hard length against Lia, Araton lowered his head and murmured in her ear, "Hold on tight, Dove." Araton turned his head and claimed her lips in a searing kiss at the same moment that he teleported them to Heaven.

Several long seconds later he broke away from her mouth and gazed into her passion filled eyes. Something nagged at the back of his mind, but he was too busy calming his need to focus on it.

Licking her lips, Lia's green eyes shifted over his shoulder. "Holy…is this Heaven?"

"Yes, this is the mystical realm called Heaven," he countered with a quirk. He wondered what she thought their surroundings.

"I thought for sure I'd be rejected at the gate. I guess I'm meant to be here," she observed as she looked around.

Araton smiled and twined their hands together. "It's fate," he blurted.

He'd never given it much thought, but suddenly knew it was true. Fate had a reason for everything. She was also a powerful entity that was tasked with helping keep the balance of existence in check.

"Fate is my new best friend," Lia countered as her gaze roamed around them. "This looks so much like any small town I've seen on Earth. Well, except the buildings are all white. But the park and the lake and the trees. It could be anywhere."

"Where do you think God got the idea from?" Araton asked with a chuckle.

"I can't believe where we live was made using Heaven as an example. It makes me want to work so much harder to save it," Lia countered. "The biggest difference is that here everything is pristine and clean where Earth is full of pollution and filth."

"We don't have the same technology to ruin our air quality here. But it's not all like a church here. Let me show you Bladz. Our bar. I used to spend a lot of time there," Araton countered.

"Heaven has a bar?"

"And, a bakery and café," he replied with a laugh. Pulling her to the left, Araton guided her up the path to the stone building. The windows were stained glass and had been gorgeous at one point, but now they fit the feel of the place. Dirty and grimy.

"It's very reassuring to see not everything in Heaven is perfect," Lia teased.

Araton loved the bar. It didn't matter to him there was layer upon layer of grit covering everything. It was one of the few places where he could both let his hair down and find a release when needed. Fights and whiskey were usually what relaxed him. Not females.

The crack of balls splitting as a cue connected with a ball settled Araton's nerves the second he opened the door. Looking around he noticed several Angels of Retribution playing a game of pool in the corner. Spheres scattered across green velvet. A blue striped ball rolled into a side pocket.

Araton glanced around and noticed angels mixing with various other supernaturals. Bladz was the one place in Heaven supes could portal into. They weren't allowed to venture outside these walls, but many visited regardless. It was hard to tell precisely who the angels were if you didn't know them because wings had to be hidden in the bar. The owner, Thorne declared them off limits. He claimed it made it difficult to see every corner of the place and when beings became intoxicated shit went south.

Bar fights broke out even in Heaven, and Thorne refused to replace anymore tables and chairs. Besides if too much shit went down there the archangels would be more likely to shut the place down. They'd reluctantly allowed him to open the joint as a safe refuge for their kind.

"This place is like something I would find on Earth," Lia said as she glanced around. Looking at him from her perspective he understood her awe. Most humans thought of his home realm as a place of mists, joy and spirits. "Should we get a drink?"

Nodding, Araton guided her to a stool. "Araton," Thorne said in greeting. The angel had been injured battling demons and when his wings never healed, he retired and opened the bar. He'd always been a hard male. His short black hair might look like it was military style, but his tattoos told another story. He had one foot on the wild side at all times.

Araton clapped Thorne's forearm and gestured to Lia. "This is Natalia. She's a human cop."

Narrowing his brown eyes, Thorne said, "Good to meet you. Welcome to Bladz," Thorne said while he assessed her. Araton wondered what the powerful angel saw in her. Thorne might run a bar now, but he was powerful and capable of seeing what most couldn't. "You're surprisingly strong. I shouldn't be surprised. Not many would be able to handle the possession of Lucifer. So, what'll it be?"

"What?" Lia blurted as she glanced around without really seeing anything. "I can't stay here," Lia blurted and jumped from the chair then raced for the door. Araton followed suit and waved to Thorne. The nervous energy left in Lia's wake told him precisely how frightened she was at the moment. And it made her move fast. She was out the door faster than he thought possible.

"Dove, stop. There's no reason to rush away like that," Araton called after her.

"Of course, there is," she hissed. "They know what I am. I've killed for no fucking reason. I'm evil and disgusting."

Araton stopped her on the path and cupped her cheek. "That was not you. Lucifer is the demon here. Figuratively and literally. You have nothing to apologize for. I've never met anyone as selfless and courageous as you. Every single day that goes by that you astonish me."

"Man, your life must be boring and uneventful," she teased with a smile.

"It was pitiful until I met you," he admitted and claimed her lips. The second his mouth moved over hers, desire blazed through his body like an inferno. He lost himself in her mouth. His hands roamed up the sides of her body then her back.

"You are now the most important. You and I have built this fortress. One night, we could make it all right. There's no need to run. Ooh," Abraxos crooned, making Araton break the kiss. Araton didn't listen to much music so he never knew what his brother was belting, but he could read between the lines on this one. He was insinuating what Lia meant to Araton. Worst part was he couldn't really argue with the lyrics.

"Brother," Araton said in greeting as he wrapped his arm around Lia's waist and pulled her close. "What are you up to?"

"I was going to pick up some cupcakes from Kara's place. I can see you have all the treats you need," Abraxos replied with a wink to Lia.

Blushing furiously, she averted her gaze to Sweet Indulgence. The bakery was close to the café and unmistakable. The neon purple sign announced it, but it was the massive windows showing the colorful tables and displays of cakes, scones and cookies that really drew the eye.

"We will see you later," Araton informed his brother and headed in the direction of his house.

"You live near here?" She asked.

"Not far. Just through the park," he told her as they walked. He pointed out the white marble archangel building to the right. And waved to several angels as they walked. By the time they reached his front door Lia had relaxed greatly.

Shutting them inside his house, Araton was glad he had his brothers set the scene. He never would have thought of the candles. His contribution before was gathering items an Abraxos's behest. It paid off to have a brother who was as familiar with females as Abraxos.

Lia gasped and looked around with her hand over her mouth. "Do you have magic and you never told me?"

"No magic. I had help," he murmured as he gathered her in his arms and lifted her.

Wrapping her arms around his neck, she crossed her feet behind his back pressing his hardening shaft against her core. "I have to be honest. I expected you to live in a cloud."

He chuckled and pressed a kiss to her lips but didn't sink into her mouth. "Not quite, but I imagine my taste seems just as bland as a cloud would. Although instead of white I use greys."

"I can help spice the place up," she offered with a kiss.

"Anytime," he agreed against her mouth. Much like Ayil, Araton had never brought another female to this home. He hadn't slept with another angel for a long time. Ever since his sister had been cheated on by her ex.

In addition to the candles spread throughout the room, his brothers had added a tray of chocolate strawberries and what smelled like Cajun food for dinner. He wasn't hungry for food at the moment but appreciated that he'd be able to feed Lia without leaving after he fucked her senseless.

Araton carried her down the hall and kicked his bedroom door open then crossed to his bed. After throwing her onto the bed he leaned over her. "I'm not sure I can be gentle. My need to fuck you is too great right now," he whispered as he tugged the shirt aside and kissed her shoulder.

Sparkling green eyes entranced and captured him. A slow smile lifted her lips and she pushed her hands under his shirt then shoved the material up his chest. The smile turned wicked and she laughed as he tugged the fabric over his head.

A groan burst from his mouth when she ran her nails over his chest and nipples. Watching the weight of her possession lift even more made something click inside his mind. He knew at that moment his highest priority was to make sure she lived a life full of pleasure and happiness. She'd more than earned it.

"Who asked you to be gentle? I need you to fuck me hard and fast," she announced as she kicked off her shoes.

Araton watched as Lia sat up then removed her shirt and jeans. His mouth went dry as her curves were revealed. She laid back down in only her bra and underwear. They weren't anything fancy, but even the pink cotton was sexy on her. Bending one knee, Lia brought one of her legs up then reached for the waist of his pants.

Popping the button with one hand, he allowed her to push the fabric to his feet. Her hands ran up his sides then she lifted her head and pressed her lips to his. Meeting her halfway, his lips moved over hers while he kicked off his boots. The sexual energy between them made him fumble in his haste to get his pants off.

His need was at a fever pitch as he hovered over her and kissed a path down the side of her neck. His lips zinged, making him groan. He hovered over her breasts, running his tongue along the edge of the fabric. Her panting breaths was music to his ears. Unable to stop himself, he pushed her bra down and freed her nipple. His tongue danced an erotic rhythm over the pearled tip and made his cock hard as stone.

Lifting his head, he went back to her mouth. His lips moved over hers, and her back arched, making her nipples press into his chest. It made his balls draw up tight. He needed to be inside her and forced himself to go slower than last time. She deserved more from him than hurried rutting.

Araton reached behind them and unbuttoned her bra. Breaking the kiss, he gazed down at her. She lifted her hand and when she touched the top of his wing, he realized he lost control of keeping them hidden. Closing his eyes, he tried to calm enough to make them disappear.

"No. Leave them out. I love seeing them," she told him.

Nodding, he pressed his lips to hers again and leaned on one elbow. With his free hand he pinched her nipples.

"I thought you weren't going to be gentle. This is torture. I need you inside me," she begged and arched her back. He couldn't help but break from her mouth to kiss a path down her body. He sucked, licked and laved her nipples for several minutes before moving on.

When he reached her underwear, Araton pushed the cotton fabric down and tugged them off her legs. Her sweet scent intensified, filling the air. His fingers roamed between her legs and slid through her arousal.

"It's excruciating to go slow, but I can't keep from exploring your perfection."

With a smile, she spread her legs, putting her wet slit on display. That was all it took to make him lose all semblance of going slow. "Fuck." Transfixed, Araton rubbed her clit and his mouth lowered to her bellybutton. It was more difficult than he thought to pause and make sure she was ready for him.

"Right there," she instructed him. A moan left her mouth and her hips lifted. She was chasing his hand as he moved it away.

Giving into her silent request, he pressed harder and let her move. Her breasts bounced with her movements as she rode his hand, taking what she needed. There was nothing sexier than Lia claiming her pleasure. Her movements increased and her arousal flooded his hand. Knowing she was close Araton inserted a finger into her core and groaned when her body clenched around his digit.

Lowering his head, Araton sucked a nipple into his mouth at the same time he pumped his fingers in and out of her. He pressed his thumb against her clit. A hoarse shout of his name exploded from her mouth and a second later she detonated.

"Fuck me," she panted.

"Anything you want, Dove."

Hot fingers brushed his lower abdomen, making him gasp and look down. He saw his fingers glisten with her arousal when he removed them from her sheath and her small hand pushed the fabric of his boxer briefs down, freeing his shaft.

He lifted up so it was easier for her to push the cotton down his legs. Once he kicked them off, he returned to the bed and nudged her legs apart. Something inside melted and reshaped at the image she made. The heat in her eyes, the way her arousal glistened in the candlelight and the smile she gave him.

His arousal beaded on the head of his cock. He gripped his erection and slid it through her folds, coating his length in her arousal. The contact made her hips shoot toward him. There was no need for him to explain that move.

"You are sexy and perfect. Allow Heaven's energy inside along with my cock," he urged her.

"Anything as long as you fuck me," Lia begged.

Araton lowered his torso closer to hers and kissed the corner of her mouth. When she turned her head and his lips met hers, he thrust balls deep into her core in one hard stroke. He nearly lost his seed when she cried out and her muscles clamped down on him.

There was no way to stop himself from setting up an urgent rhythm. The urgency of their combined need obliterated every other thought. She was human and he should be careful, but the thought popped into his head and vanished with each sensual stroke. This female was more addictive than cocaine for humans.

Sweat broke across her skin as their bodies moved together. His wings expanded out to the sides, drawing her touch. Her hands roamed over the feathers before she wrapped them around his back.

Her fingers teased the wing slits where they came out of his back. He quickened his pace, chasing after what they both desperately needed. When he couldn't move more than short, shallow thrusts into her body because she'd clamped down on his cock, he knew they'd reach climax soon.

Pulling all of his Light, he added it to the seed building up in his body. He wanted to tell her he loved her and ask if she would mate him, but he kept his mouth shut and reached between their bodies to rub her clit.

Lia bit down on his shoulder as her orgasm exploded. He hoped she marked his skin like she'd done to his heart and soul. Nothing felt as good as losing himself in Natalia's perfect body. After two more thrusts, Araton stopped moving as he climaxed.

"I love you," he blurted.

She gazed at him with wide eyes but said nothing. It was a good thing that a second later the force of his orgasm made his back arch as light shot from his body with his seed. He couldn't look at her right then. He hadn't meant to say anything.

Bright light surrounded them as he collapsed above her and held her close. He prayed this was enough to keep Lucifer from taking the wheel again. His Lia wouldn't hesitate to eliminate the threat the Lord of the Underworld posed, even if it meant taking her own life. The safety of others was paramount for her. It was one of the things he loved about her.

The fact that he loved her was an astonishing revelation. He braced himself for her rejection. Knowing her she would think he was saying it to save her life. Problem was she wouldn't be entirely wrong. He couldn't let Lucifer torment her anymore. It would devastate him if he lost her. Good thing he hadn't asked her to mate him. That would have sealed his fate. He'd woo and court her and win her over.

You're going to be too late. The admonition chilled his blood. He had to save her. Pressing a kiss to her forehead, he urged her to get up and draped a robe around her shoulders. "Let's get you some dinner. I don't know about you, but I've worked up an appetite."

"Araton..." she said and let her voice trail off.

Pressing a kiss to her lips, he shook his head. "There is no need for you to say anything. I just needed to let you know how I feel. Now, let's eat," he encouraged her.

"Thank you for taking me here and making love to me. I feel as if a hundred-pound weight has been lifted from my shoulders," she replied as she grabbed his hand and headed to the kitchen.

"Good because after I feed you, I'm going to infuse you with more of my light," he told her then grabbed her ass, making her squeal. Laughing, she ran from the room and he followed. Her laughter was almost enough to banish the disappointment sitting like a stone in his gut.

Despite his words he would have liked to hear she had fallen for him, as well. He needed to remind himself loving her and giving her something good to hold onto was what mattered. Without it she would succumb to Lucifer.

*L*ia reread the report, telling herself to concentrate this time. The words blurred as her mind went back to her time in Heaven with Araton. She was falling for the angel. Big time. He was impulsive and jumped in without thinking. And she discovered she loved that about him.

He didn't overthink things. Sometimes he didn't think it through beyond killing the enemy and destroying their assets, but it wasn't entirely a bad thing. From everything she had learned lately, her angel's actions were usually taken to protect innocent humans and supernaturals.

Lia on the other hand over analyzed everything. For a split second after Araton professed his love to her she wanted to say the same thing back to him. And then the knowledge that she was tainted barged into her mind and kept her mouth shut.

She was falling for the angel. It seemed impossible, but it was as if lightning had struck the moment they met. There was scarcely a second that passed without her thinking about Araton. That was an understatement.

She was obsessed with her angel. Always wondering what he was doing. Wishing she'd had more time in Heaven to meet his parents and discover more about where he came from. It was still shocking that there was a bar there. And a café. Seeing what little she had explained his surliness. Angels weren't cherubs flying around bestowing happiness and love on people.

Some might be. But they were just as prone to anger as anyone. And their warriors were badasses that carried flaming swords. Given the stories about the war that divided heaven she shouldn't have been so surprised to learn some angels were highly skilled killers.

"What's wrong? Did you find something?" Araton asked.

Lia titled her head to him and gave him a small smile. "Just thinking about last night."

Araton's tense shoulders relaxed and he smirked at her then bent and placed a kiss to her lips. Pulling back he murmured, "I would have thought you'd have a smile on those pouty lips after the night we had. Perhaps I need to fuck you senseless again."

Arousal flooded Natalia and made her core clench. Her body knew the pleasure he could deliver and wanted more. "I wouldn't object to that, but I promised I would search the database for any hints about where the archdemon might be."

With a groan, Araton kissed her one more time then straightened. "As much as I want to drag you to my bed upstairs, we need to find that asshole. My brothers and the Dark Warriors found no sign when they cleaned out the stadium. Given the plans they overheard we need to act fast."

"I would agree. I haven't been involved long, but it seems like the demons have been escalating their efforts. How is Izzy handling the news Lucifer wants to claim her?" Natalia hated knowing he could take possession of her. She wasn't sure what was worse. Being his victim or forced to mate with him. Both were vile possibilities.

Much to her relief she hadn't felt the darkness threatening to steal her soul since Araton had taken her to Heaven. She hoped that meant his efforts strengthened her and made it possible to cut Lucifer off. She'd been too terrified to poke much at the dark orb she knew sat silently in her chest. The last time she did that she blacked out and woke up after almost killing Aison.

"Izzy is pissed about being forced back to Zeum. She believed she was off the demon radar and isn't taking to being cooped up very well," Araton told her.

"Did they say they could still feel her like you said they used to be able to? It's one thing to be told not to harm her because Lucy wants her to become the Queen of the Underworld, but I would still think demons would flock to her energy."

Araton caressed her cheek. "You're right. I don't think they can find her like they used to. I don't think her parents are keeping her home for the same reasons as before."

"Makes sense. Even more reason to find the fucker tormenting my city and eliminate him," Lia said as she went back to scanning police reports. Searching through every homicide, she stopped at one in the Garden District not far from the house she was currently sitting in. "Hey look at this."

Araton put his cell phone down and scanned the report she'd pulled up. "What made you stop on this one? It seems like a typical case of domestic violence. The husband killed his wife then shot himself."

"The wound doesn't fit with a gunshot. Can demons thrall humans?"

Araton lifted one eyebrow then turned back and reread the report. "Okay. You've got my attention. Archdemons are upper level demons and capable of far more than lesser ones. I believe that might be possible, but why? It doesn't make sense."

Lia shrugged as she considered all of the information she'd learned in the past week and a half. "Very few of your neighbors would commit such a crime. Yes, they can be abusive, but not many of them would take their own lives. And even if they could, they wouldn't cut out their own heart with a steak knife which is the only thought that comes to mind when I read that report."

"You have a point, but why go to all these lengths? It doesn't fit their MO to take what they want when they want," Araton replied.

"The luxury?" She suggested then really thought about his question. He was right. Demons didn't need to plan a coverup and go to the trouble of hiding their actions. "If they can stay off your radar along with the Dark Warriors they can act longer. They're in this for the bigger goal, right? Perhaps they set up the stadium and all the other rituals to keep you off their trail while they gathered power for the final spell."

Jumping to his feet, Araton snatched his phone from the table. "You're right. They've been keeping us distracted with one hand while hoarding the energy in the other. I know we dealt them a blow by releasing the spirits from that house. They haven't been able to collect a significant amount of energy from that location. We've not left it unattended long enough for them to return."

Lia watched him type out a message before he picked her up and crushed her in a hug. His mouth descended on hers a second later. She opened when he licked her lower lip. A moan left her as his tongue danced with hers.

Her hands clutched his broad shoulders and held tight. One of his hands slipped beneath her shirt and teased the flesh of her lower back. His touch was electric and sent zaps of energy arching through her blood along with desire for more.

She was about to wrap one leg around his hip so she could rub her clit against his shaft when his phone pinged with a response. Cursing, he broke the kiss and picked up the device. "My brother's will meet us at the house, along with Dante and the others."

"Will Aison be there?" She wanted to apologize to him for nearly killing him.

"Yes. The skin and muscles around his shoulder have healed and he is ready to get his revenge."

Lia twined her fingers with Araton's and followed him to this backyard. He pressed a kiss to her lips, and she felt her skin tingling from more than banked arousal. He was turning them invisible.

His wings were magnificent as they expanded and flapped rapidly. She held on tight as they lifted into the air. The night below them was quiet and peaceful. When they landed in the yard of the house that had seen violence two weeks ago, she thought she was mistaken about her hunch.

"What if I'm wrong?"

"You're not," he whispered as he glanced around.

Together they snuck up to the front porch. It was similar to the one at Les Augres Manor with massive white columns holding up the roof and an old wood bench off to the side of the double front doors.

She ducked when she saw movement through the large window. Sheer curtains hid details, but there was no doubt someone was inside the house. Pulling her gun from the back of her pants, she held it down by her thigh.

Araton looked back at her and motioned to the front door. The glass was frosted to obscure the inside, so she had no idea precisely what they were walking into, but she trusted her angel.

Keeping close, she followed him as tested the knob. Surprisingly, it was unlocked and they were heading inside before anyone else arrived. The second they entered chaos erupted.

Demons ran down the stairs and chilling laughter echoed from the parlor to the left of the entryway. Araton called his flaming sword to his hand and started swinging. Heads literally rolled with each swipe of his weapon. Turning her back to him, she focused on the demon in the parlor.

A handsome man walked out with a smile on his face. She lifted her gun and pulled the trigger. The guy jerked back, and black blood spurted from his chest the second her bullets penetrated.

"Get out of here, Dove. It's not safe for you," Araton shouted as he continued to slash and slay.

"I'm not leaving you," she vowed.

"How sweet. I know Lucifer would prefer you to stay when he takes over so he can kill the angel," the good-looking demon replied. Lia's blood froze in her veins with his words.

No way would she ever be the death of Araton. She lifted her hand to point her gun at her own head and screamed when a loafer kicked her wrist. The bone snapped and her gun went flying.

Araton was surrounded by hellhounds and countless other demons while the attractive archdemon prowled closer to her. She went to run like Araton had told her, but that placid dark orb in her chest burst open and enveloped her like a tidal wave.

As her vision wavered, Lia held onto thoughts of her angel and staying with him. She refused to be the reason he died. A cry left her as her body collapsed to the ground.

There was no doubt the stabbing pain in her head was from Lucifer trying to take the wheel.

"Fuck you," she spat. It wasn't happening this time. Araton believed in her and she was going to prove he was right to place his bets on her and not the devil.

She tried to fight when the archdemon picked her up, but she couldn't let up on her battle against Lucifer. Not even when she heard her angel scream. The last thing she saw before the world around her vanished was his brothers and the Dark Warriors bursting through the front door to join the battle.

She reached for Araton praying that she could fight the Dark Lord long enough to return to her angel. She should have told him she loved him when she'd had the chance. Her life couldn't end like this without telling him he'd made her believe in love at first sight.

CHAPTER 19

"*Lia!*" He shouted and slashed his sword frantically. The fucking archdemon just disappeared with her in his clutches. It was plainly obvious right before he took her that Lucifer tried to take control of his Dove and she was fighting his possession.

"What is it, brother?" Abraxos asked when he appeared a second later.

Araton swiveled and swung his weapon of Light through the bodies of the two demons closest to him. "The archdemon set a trap and took Natalia. They ambushed me and separated us. She was fighting Lucifer when they disappeared."

"Fucking hell," Abraxos blurted as he joined the fight.

Ayil had arrived when Araton was explaining what happened and jumped in with his weapon. "We need to find them before they get any further with their goal."

"Ya think?" Araton muttered then cursed when a rage demon sliced through his left bicep. With a snarl, Araton cut its head off and kicked it at a Sheti demon. Those fuckers smelled like rotting ass and looked like lizard men. They were some of the vilest beings that existed. Mainly due to their smell but also because they could withstand more than most of their kind.

Dante and the Dark Warriors were on scene a few minutes later and they made quick work of the remaining enemies stalling Araton's departure. The archdemon knew neither he nor his brothers could leave a contingent this large to go chasing after him and Lia. And it was killing Araton that his duty to the humans was interfering with him rescuing her.

If Gabriel got wind of this, the archangel would not hesitate to kill Natalia to eliminate the threat she posed and cut off all possibility for Lucifer to use her to gain freedom. But there was no way he would ever allow that to happen. Lia was his everything.

He had no idea when it all changed for him, but he was done denying how he felt. He loved her more than reason and he was going to do what he did best. Act on his impulses. Thank God today that was rescuing Lia and mating with her, sending Lucifer back to Hell with no hope for parole.

Sure, the Dark Lord had gotten a taste of freedom and he would want more, but the situation with Natalia was unique. He'd been thinking for a week about how Lucifer managed to possess her when every other attempt had failed.

Unfortunately, Araton's rash actions were to blame. His blood had not only kept her alive, but it also strengthened Natalia to be able to survive the powerful possession. It was her strong personality that refused to allow complete control that minimized the damage Lucifer could do through her.

It made Araton love her even more. There wasn't a more perfect female alive. And, he was going to tell her that. But first he had to find her.

Cutting the head from the last hellhound, Araton released his sword and bent at the knees. Sweat beaded his brow and his heart raced in his tight chest. The smell of charred demon hung heavy in the air making him want to hurl, but it was the fact that he could hardly catch his breath that bothered him. And it had little to do with the battle he'd just waged.

There was no room in his mind for anything except Natalia. She needed him and he was going to be there for her.

"We need to find her. Now!" Araton demanded.

"There is nothing we can do until we find where the archdemon took her," Ayil told him as he clapped him on the shoulder.

Araton was shaking his head, ready to argue for taking action immediately when Dante cut him off. "We have to clean this scene up before we go anywhere. Humans will lose their fucking minds if they come across this shit."

"He's right," Abraxos cut in. Lifting his right hand to his side, Abraxos had his flaming sword in his grip a second later. Without waiting for a reply, he started cutting into dead carcasses.

Ayil joined in and reluctantly so did Araton. Many of the demons had been turned to ash by the angelic weapons wielded by him and his brothers. He should be concerned about cleaning up the rest of the mess, but he could think of nothing but reaching Lia before it was too late. His churning gut told him she was close to losing the battle against Lucifer forever.

Needing a distraction, he sliced into the dead bodies forcing his flame through them. "Were you able to find any information?" Araton asked Dante.

The Cambion Lord shook his head as he kicked parts towards him and his brothers. "There were rumors about the

Dark Lord having returned. Of course, we know that's true. I didn't learn anything more. But I got the impression they were here in New Orleans. Everything seemed to hinge on the energy from this city's history."

"That makes sense," Araton said as he stored his blade and lifted his arm to check the injury to his bicep. It was still bleeding, and the flesh gaped open half an inch. It ached but wouldn't slow him down. He doubted anything would at this point. The determination to save Lia increased with each passing minute.

"They've been putting more effort into this area. There are archdemons all across the world casting spells, but fellow Warriors have reported a decrease in activity in recent days," Araton continued.

"What does that mean?" Aison asked as he rubbed the shoulder that Lia nearly sliced clean through days ago. He imagined it still bothered the shifter. An injury like he suffered might heal quickly, but there was usually lingering discomfort. Araton had been injured enough times to know how that worked.

"It means that demons saw success here and efforts concentrated in our fair city," Luke interjected.

"Precisely. They aren't likely to start over new somewhere else until we free Lia from her connection to the Dark Lord," Araton added. "We need to be prepared to launch an attack on the archdemon as soon as we locate Lia."

"If history tells us anything, the seven of us will not be enough to beat him. I think we need to call Zander and Hayden in for reinforcements," Dante suggested.

"You contact them and bring as many Dark Warriors as you can. I'd ask for more Warrior Angels, but if Gabriel discovers what happened he will come and kill Natalia. And I will never let that happen," Araton vowed.

Ayil clapped his hand on Araton's shoulder. "We won't allow you to lose her," his brother promised.

Abraxos nodded then sang, "Don't give it up, don't say it hurts. 'Cause there's nothing like this feeling, baby. Now that I found you. I want it all. No, there's nothing like this feeling, baby."

Araton punched his brother in the arm and flared his wings. "Let's meet up in one hour at Les Augres. I'm going to search the city for signs of where she could have been taken."

"You'd better not go after her if you find her," Ayil told him.

"I won't," Araton replied. No fucking way was he going to wait if he located Natalia. He would do anything to save her. Even if that cost him his life. A hand on his shoulder stopped him from taking off.

"I mean it, brother," Ayil growled. "Rushing in without back up will cost her life. I know you love her. Trust me, you will never recover if you do something stupid that costs her life. If there is ever a time for you to think before you act, now is that moment."

It was the only thing that Araton would have heard with his current state of mind. He could hardly think about anything for more than a split second before it went right back to thinking of Lia.

"Fucker," Araton cursed at his brother. "I won't do anything without you guys. I'll see you soon." Pushing off, Araton was soaring through the air a second later.

The knot in his gut tightened and his heart raced faster as he flew. His wings beat the air harder and he went faster. With each stroke his mind churned over where she was and if Lucifer had taken over her psyche again.

Lia would never forgive herself if she killed anyone else. Not that it was her fault, but she would take the blame for not killing herself. She had a heart of gold and the courage of an angelic warrior.

Araton picked up demonic energy below him and stopped flying to hover in place. When he looked down, he saw a cemetery with the tombs he'd become acquainted with in the area. This one was larger than the one he'd visited with Lia a couple days ago.

Landing as quietly as possible, Araton kept his presence hidden. Demons would sense his angelic heritage, but there was nothing he could do about it. Creeping forward, he scanned as much as he could of his surroundings.

Dark signals drew him to the far west corner of the property. Initially, the ground was pure, and he thought he'd been mistaken about demons being present, but that changed the more he crossed the property. By the time he reached the tombs in the back the level of Dark infecting the area made him expect to see black soil.

Two Sheti demons yowled and raced from behind one of the small structures. Araton called his sword of light to his hand and decapitated one of the beasts. The other raked its claws across the back of Araton's right wing.

Executing a roundhouse kick, Araton punted the lizard away from him. By the time he stopped moving the demon was snarling and facing off with him. Needing to move on and continue his search, Araton took to the air and held his Sword of Light aloft. Right before he made contact, the Sheti leapt into the air and came at him.

The move startled Araton and he dropped his sword. It disappeared before making it very far. Angelic weapons went back to their hiding spot the second they left their owner's hand. That way no one except an angel could wield it.

The demon had grabbed hold of Araton so that it didn't fall right back to the ground. Claws sliced his shoulder, leaving behind three deep cuts. The Sheti screeched loudly when Araton's blood splattered its scaly skin.

Taking advantage, Araton threw the beast to the ground and called his weapon to his hand again. He was flying over the demon and slicing through the thick neck before it even knew what hit it.

Araton continued on, leaving the remnants to burn to ash. He made a mental note to have angels reclaim every inch of the resting place. There was no way to know when anyone would be buried in those back tombs and he refused to leave the demons anymore spots of power if he could help it.

Araton flew over the city and encountered two more demons, but never discovered where the archdemon was amassing his forces for the next ritual. Araton's nerves jangled and he was ready to beg Gabriel to ask God for help.

Surely, He would be able to locate the archdemon. Humans had countless stories of Him being omniscient, but Araton had never bothered to verify that claim. Honestly, he had no idea how anyone being could be. No matter how powerful.

It seemed an impossible task to be able to function while having incalculable streams of information clogging the mind. While he didn't believe God was omniscient, he did believe He had powers that could locate Natalia so Araton could save her.

The fact that Araton suspected Lia would be killed if Gabriel discovered her current condition was the only thing that stopped him from seeking help. Heading to Les Augres, Araton gave himself until morning before he sought more help. He just hoped Gabriel would be willing to accept Araton's sacrifice to save Natalia if it came to that.

Landing on the lawn of the manor, he approached the front door and knocked. Aison opened the panel with a nod. "Good that you showed up. I was just about to call you and your brothers. Zander and Hayden are here. I believe they have some information."

Araton's heart leaped in his chest while hope soared. He half expected there to be an Angel of Hope when he entered the stately mansion with how powerful the emotion was at hearing those words.

"I'll text my brothers," he said as he followed the shifter to the war room. He pulled out his phone and typed a message to both of his siblings informing them to return to the Dark Warrior headquarters in NOLA. "Did someone find the archdemon?"

"No' yet," Zander called out from the room. Araton had asked Aison, but the Vampire King answered before his warrior was able.

"Good to see you again," Hayden greeted then extended his hand. The male had shaggy brown hair and dark brown eyes. As the leader of all shifters, the Omega was a massive guy. From what Araton had been told, Hayden could shift into any animal. He was the only one of the shifters with this ability.

"Thank you for coming to help," Araton told the Omega. "What's this new information?"

"There's nothing concrete, yet," Zander responded and waved to the television on the opposite wall. It was on and showed the war room back at Zeum. "We have Killian with us via Skype. He's been doing some research based on what we've discovered over the past couple weeks."

Araton nodded to the Alliance member. He noticed Jace, Bhric and Izzy were with him in the room in Seattle. Kyran, Mack, Rhys and Gerrick were at Les Augres with them. He appreciated the show of support.

"Given how many sites you all have been interrupting, I suggested he look outside the Quarter," Evzen interjected as he poked his head in from the side of the screen. "They cannot use the sites you guys have been cleansing and reclaiming, so they will need a new source of energy."

"Based on that suggestion, I've looked at likely spots. The most viable one is just downriver at the Chalmette Battlefield," Killian explained via the online connection. "The archdemon will need the energy of death to fuel their final spell. That site was where a famous battle took place. Lucifer's goons have been gaining power with each ritual done in and around the French Quarter, but those are no longer available like Evzen said. At Chalmette, countless soldiers lost their lives a couple hundred years ago."

"Is there a way we can look remotely?" Araton asked. All too often he forgot about modern technology and how it can help in situations like this. He didn't know the history of the city, but a location like this would be prime grounds for demonic activity.

"I have Luke and Slate on their way to the location as we speak. They will let us know what they find when they get there," Zander explained.

"If this doesn't pan out, we need to call in the human police force. They already have officers spread throughout the area. It will be far easier than doing a grid search," Hayden interjected.

Araton's throat went dry with the Omega's suggestion and his heart pounded even harder in his chest. That was the worst idea he'd ever heard. Araton wanted to find Lia more than anything but giving more power for Lucifer to take over was not going to make things easier for them.

"Humans can't help in this situation. They'd only be offering themselves up as sacrifices to fuel the archdemon's spell. We would never reach her in time. I will not risk my mate's life in this," Araton blurted. He decided to leave the rest of the reason involving humans was a bad idea. They didn't have time to argue the matter right now.

"Araton is right," Dante agreed.

Abraxos and Ayil walked in a second later and were filled in on the current situation. By the time they were done being updated, Zander's phone pinged with an incoming call.

"Can you send this through the call, Kill? They are Face-timing me and I'd rather everyone see so I doona have to play go between," Zander asked.

"Sure thing. One second," Killian replied as he typed on the keyboard in front of him. A second later an expansive lawn was on the screen.

"Slate. Are you there?" Zander called out.

"We're here. And so are the demons. See that obelisk that's glowing dark red? It was white when we arrived," Slate replied.

"And not glowing," Luke added. "My skin feels like it's being stabbed by thousands of man-sized wasps right now."

Araton's stomach churned as he watched the pulsing of the tall building. He noticed countless creatures prowling around the base, but the warriors were too far away for him to get a clear picture. He didn't need to see more to know they were demons. Not only did Luke's description of what he was feeling fit perfectly with a demonic presence, Araton could practically feel the evil through the connection.

"Let's go," he demanded and turned to walk out of the room. Abraxos and Ayil were next to him.

"We need a few minutes to get organized," Zander informed him. Araton nodded but ignored the orders Zander barked behind him.

There was a ticking bomb in his mind. Each second was one closer to him losing Lia forever. The power in that building told him there would be no coming back from it for her if they didn't act fast. If they were indeed too late, Araton would make it his life's mission to kill every demon he could.

Getting vengeance for Natalia would be the only thing that kept him going. He didn't want to live without her, but he refused to leave this life until he avenged her. She deserved at least that from him since he wasn't able to protect her from the rest.

raton landed next to the Luke and Slate. His brothers landed right next to him. The two Dark Warriors were huddled near the dock were boats arrived. They faced the street where the others would arrive and had a good view of the property in question.

The water was behind them and in the distance, he saw trees and what looked like a plantation house complete with at least seven white columns along the front. The balcony on the second floor seemed to have furniture on it, but he couldn't be sure.

There was another building and then the focal point. The large obelisk shaped building that was pulsing with a dark red light. The thing was obviously the focal point of the ritual.

It took him running a mantra on a repeated loop that he couldn't face the archdemon and its minions through his head to stop him from rushing headlong to save Lia. It helped that he sensed her somewhere close by. He had to believe that if she'd already lost her fight with Lucifer that he wouldn't sense her at all.

Scanning what he could see in front of them, he catalogued the line of trees closest to the river. Aside from the three buildings there were a couple of old cannons in the large field, but nothing else.

The demons didn't have the advantage on this one. They would instinctively stay away from the river. Running water weakened them. That left the plantation house, the other low building and the tall obelisk.

"Have you seen any sign of Lia?" Araton asked. Yes, he sensed her, but he needed to know she was okay more than he needed to breathe.

Slate glanced over his shoulder and shook his head. "Not a sign. But we've counted at least three dozen demons coming through a portal next to the tree in front of the house."

For several long, agonizing minutes Araton worried he might have made a mistake by not going to Gabriel or even calling on other Warrior Angels for help with this mission. There had never been more on the line than there was at this moment.

He finally understood why Ayil risked for much for Kennex. For months he'd assumed his brother had lost his mind. Not that Araton hated Kennex or anything. Initially he'd been wary of her and encouraged his brother to take more action against her and her kind, but once it was discovered that she wasn't aligned with demons he was fine with her. But he hadn't really comprehended what Ayil had gone through or felt until now.

The demons roamed restlessly around the lawn in front of the tall spire but didn't make a move to do anything else. Araton wondered what they were waiting for and nearly took to the air to do a little reconnaissance when Zander and the Dark Warriors pulled up.

The benefit of cooperating with supernaturals trained in

combat was that they got organized and were ready to approach the demons within seconds. Good thing too because Araton couldn't stay back any longer.

"Kyran, you and your team approach from the south. I will take the west while Aison and his group come in from the north. Araton if you and your brothers can carry Slate, Aison and Gerrick then fly over to the east then we will all be in place to attack at the same time," Zander instructed.

"Sounds good. Let's go," Araton replied as he motioned to Gerrick. He wanted the ruthless warrior at his side.

"Don't drop me, 'kay? Shae and I have a date tomorrow night that I don't want to miss. Izzy's watching Maddox so it'll just be us," Gerrick told him with a smirk.

Araton chuckled. The sorcerer's confidence was well placed. He was one of the best fighters Araton had ever met. Gerrick's skill made risk of injury minimal for him. "I'll do my best. Thanks for helping," Araton told everyone.

There were nods and grunts as he lifted into the air a few feet and then grabbed Gerrick under his arms. It took Araton a moment to stabilize his grip before he took off over the land and to the other side where they would approach the horde.

Less than a minute later he and Gerrick landed, followed by his brothers, Aison and Slate. The six of them crouched in the trees. They weren't very far from the gathering demons.

"Are those people they're dragging toward the tall building?" Gerrick whispered so low Araton had to lean close to hear the warrior.

Araton's gut clenched when he noticed Gerrick was right. He saw at least a dozen men and women in demon clutches. It was impossible to tell from this distance if they were human or supernatural. Or even alive, he realized with a start. All had obvious injuries and were bleeding. At least one had to be dead given the large gash across his abdomen.

"Yes. We go in now. We can't allow them to kill all those innocents," Araton growled. Gerrick nodded while the others looked in the directions the others would attack from.

Araton didn't bother waiting for approval. They were there and humans were going to kill them if they hadn't already. Lifting off, Araton arrowed toward the horde a foot above the ground.

He called his sword to his hand at the last minute and was able to decapitate at least three demons, one Sheti and two hellhounds, before the others realized they were under attack.

Gerrick and the others were right behind him and jumped right into battle alongside Araton. It was a challenge to get a good look at the entire scene and Araton couldn't lift into the air just yet.

Rushing toward a pus demon that was holding a man, he swung his weapon, but the demon ducked out of the way. The fist that connected with his head was surprisingly solid. He guessed it was only the mid-section of the pus monster that was soft and squishy. Or could they solidify parts of their anatomy at will?

The answer didn't actually matter. Darting in close, Araton released his sword of light and snatched his dagger from the sheath at his back. With a swift motion, he stabbed through pus and encountered bones. When the demon's grip on his victim lessened, Araton was relieved to hear the grunt as the guy dropped to the ground.

Switching his dagger to his other hand, Araton called his sword back to his hand and was slicing through the pus demon's middle less than a heartbeat later. Dipping down, Araton slashed his flaming sword through the middle and musty, burning flesh gagged him with how close he was to the beast.

Hands grabbed his wings and pulled him down on the

ground. Claws digging into the top of his wings told Araton a demon had latched onto him. Something cracked in his left wing when he was kicked by a rage demon and then stomped on.

His grip loosened on his sword and it disappeared, but he still had his dagger and he switched it to his dominate hand. Rolling to his right to alleviate the pain on his left side, Araton kicked both feet and swung his right arm in an arch.

The dagger in his hand plunged into the leg of a rage demon. Araton was pinned with black, acidic blood dripping onto his arm where it sizzled. Gerrick's shout, drew Araton's attention along with the demons' gazes. It gave him the edge he needed. Exploding from the ground, Araton called his Sword of Light to his hand and slashed through necks and torsos.

One quick glance around told Araton they were surrounded. He couldn't see the building to his right through the bodies. All he was able to catch was the red light pulsing off the stone of the structure.

Gerrick fought next to him like a lethal wave. Araton was impressed all over again by his skill. The Dark Warrior never missed a target and little things like claws raking skin didn't distract him one bit. Araton had no idea how the male went so deep into his fighting, but he wished he'd asked before now.

Swinging his sword as he turned toward some growling to his right, Araton stepped into the move at the last second and managed to slice the front leg of a hellhound off. Where was Lia? Every now and then he was able to sense her presence and each time it came from the obelisk which was why he kept trying to look in that direction.

"Abraxos," Araton called out to his brother. "Find all the injured humans you can and take them out of the immediate area. I think they are planning on using them to power the spell."

"On it," Abraxos replied from behind him.

Araton tried to make his way toward the location he kept sensing Natalia. He didn't make it more than five feet when he was no longer able to cut his way through the enemies.

Two Sheti demons stood in his way, forcing him to pause and eliminate them before he moved on. He contemplated taking to the air, but his injury kept him grounded. Anger threatened to take over his mind, but he refused to fuel the rage demons close by. Lia was being used by the Dark Lord and these vile creatures were keeping him from helping her. The woman he loved was going to lose her life if he didn't stop this ritual from happening.

A surge in demonic energy broke something in him the second that thought popped up as if the Dark power read his mind. With a roar, Araton became a whirlwind and slashed through the demons closest to him.

Black blood burning his arms and face, Araton continued hacking his way toward Natalia. Gerrick remained close by his side, making it easier to reach his destination. After taking out several more beasts, Araton was finally able to catch a glimpse of the stairs at the base of the tall spire.

Natalia was standing at the top, bent over and screaming in pain. Her head shook from side to side and blood dribbled from her ears. Everything except her receded from his awareness.

Something solid slammed into him from the side while he was slashing and fighting his way to his mate. He landed on the ground with a thud. Bile rose in his throat as his head bounced on the bloody grass.

Thank God for training because it kept his sword arm in movement, and he was able to eliminate the Behemoth demon that had knocked him down. Araton was back on unsteady feet a racing heartbeat later.

Determined to reach her side, Araton had taken one step when he watched a massive Pus demon club the back of Gerrick's skull, making the warrior go down. "Fuck!" Araton shouted and ran to Gerrick's aide.

He could not allow the warrior to be injured or worse. Not only did Gerick have a mate and child that needed him, but the Tehrex Realm couldn't lose their best warrior. Araton's flaming sword slashed through the creatures heading toward Gerrick.

The flames of his sword were faltering after so much demonic blood coated the blade. It needed to be cleaned, but there was no time. Araton called on his angelic essence and added thoughts of Lia to fuel more powerful fire. The weapon blazed orange-red and then green like Natalia's stunning eyes.

Jumping to his feet, Gerrick joined him and they fought their way toward Natalia. By the time they reached the stairs the horde was thinning, and he was joined by his brothers, Zander and several other Dark Warriors.

"I see you're back, Azazel," Zander called out to the archdemon standing over Lia. "I thought you learned your lesson, but apparently not."

"Time to die, asshole," Araton growled as he slashed his Sword of Light through the air.

"You go to Natalia,' Zander called out to him. "We've got this one."

Nodding to Zander, Araton hurried up the steps toward Natalia. He made it within five feet of her and fell to his knees as malevolent energy buffeted him from the front. It felt as if razor blades were cutting his skin. One glance down and he saw there were thousands of small cuts all over his body.

Clenching his fists, he ignored the blood that trickled from the wounds and continued to Natalia's side. Every step was a monumental effort, but he refused to give up. If this was what she was going through, he couldn't believe she was still standing. Evil beat at him with every pulse of his heart, trying to burrow its way inside.

Araton doubted he would have been able to withstand it if he weren't trying to reach the woman who had become his entire world. Needing to reach her side gave him the strength to take each agonizing step.

"Hold on, Dove. I'm almost there," Araton called out. Natalia lifted her head and gazed at him with bright green eyes. She was now squatting with her arms wrapped around her knees and her knuckles white where she was clutching her hands together.

"I don't think I can fight this anymore. You have to kill me. I love you, Araton," she whispered. A tear slid down her cheek and she held his gaze, telling him how serious she was about him ending her life.

"I will never let you go. I'm going to mate you as soon as I get you out of here. Don't give up yet, please," he begged her. "I can't live without you."

"You want to mate me?" Lia asked. The ball of her body relaxed slightly, and her head lifted. It might be wishful thinking on his part, but he swore his words were strengthening her. And, weakening the energy cutting him to shreds.

"Yes. If you'll have me. But I need you to keep on fighting," Araton instructed her. He practically crawled the last few feet and fell at her side. His injured wing was drooping behind him and he was bleeding from multiple cuts. He needed to get them the fuck out of there, but all he could do was pull himself up next to her and wrap his arms around her trembling body.

A scream echoed behind them as the red light consuming

the building behind them disappeared. Araton lifted his head and watched as Zander struck Azazel and then both of his brothers swiped their weapons of light through the archdemon. The angelic flames consumed the demon in an instant.

"I love you, Dove," Araton told her and claimed her mouth. As his lips pressed to hers, Araton poured everything he was feeling into the kiss. Her tongue tangled with his in an intimate dance. As their passion rose, Lia trembled less, and her body unfurled for him.

Breaking away from him, Lia panted as she met his gaze. "Did you mean what you said?"

"Yes. I want to spend eternity with you, Dove. Will you mate me?" Araton asked her. With each passing second their bond got stronger and they were further from the edge of losing Lia to Lucifer.

"Yes! But I want my best friend and my family to be there. Will that be possible?"

Araton helped Lia to her feet and wrapped an arm around her waist. "There's a reason we keep our existence secret, but you've more than earned the right to have those you love by your side," he told her then turned to see that Abraxos and Ayil joined them at the top of the steps along with Zander and his Dark Warriors. "Is there someplace special you would like to get mated?"

"Your house in the Garden District would be perfect," she told him with a smile that turned to shock a second later. "I can't believe I'm marrying an angel. How did I get so lucky?"

"I'm the lucky one, Dove," he informed her then turned to his brothers. "I'm going to take her to Heaven and speak to Raphael and Gabriel. Can you guys put together a mating ceremony for three days from now? That will give Raphael time to make arrangements. I don't want to wait any longer than that." Lucifer might be suppressed right now, but he wasn't gone. He would only be gone when Araton mated Natalia.

"We can help," Zander offered. "Or rather my mate and several of the others can."

"My mom will want to help, too," Natalia interjected. Araton released the last of the fear that had driven him and listened as they made plans to connect Lia's mom and Elsie.

They almost hadn't made it in time. God might not be omniscient, but Araton had no doubt that He had helped enough to ensure their success. Sending a silent thank you to His maker, Araton gathered Lia close and teleported them to Heaven.

CHAPTER 21

Natalia checked her hair and looked over her shoulder at her best friend. Xiomara had practically throttled Lia when she told her that she was getting married and mated. She'd debated what to tell her family and closest friend about Araton and decided on the truth.

She refused to be isolated from those she loved. They were all still stunned by the fact that supernatural creatures existed, but they were there to support her nonetheless. The only piece of information she hid from them was the fact that she was going to be immortal after she mated with Araton.

They were both certain she already was. His theory was that when his blood mixed with hers through her injury that her DNA started the process and that was what allowed her to withstand Lucifer's possession which she was fighting even at that moment.

It had been one long battle for her. She wasn't able to do much aside from keep the Dark Lord at bay. Araton's sister and her friends had made minimal arrangements for them to be mated in Araton's backyard.

Many of their guests were still recovering from their injuries. Some of them had been hurt severely. When she'd seen Luke's guts hanging out of his stomach, she thought he was going to die while trying to rescue her. He promised her that he had no regrets.

Angels had surrounded her since they had returned to Araton's house two days ago. The only way to sever her connection to Lucifer was for her to mate with Araton and he wasn't taking any chances of the Dark Lord overpowering her again. Apparently, their presence weakened his connection to her.

"You ready?" Lia asked Xiomara.

"Yes. I want to see Araton's sexy brother," she replied with a waggle of her eyebrows.

"Is the archangel Raphael really performing your ceremony?" Her mom asked.

"He is," her dad replied before she could. "I just saw him arrive. Can you believe baby girl is marrying an angel, Megan?"

"Lia deserves an angel and so much more," her mom declared. "Just don't let me pass out when I meet the archangel, Doug."

"I won't let you embarrass yourself Love," her dad promised. "You look beautiful, sweetheart. You ready?"

Lia nodded and held her emotions in check. Now was not the time to break down and let the tears flow. Xiomara had spent an hour perfecting her make-up. She didn't have time to shop for a dress and had planned on wearing her nicest skirt, but her mom had surprised her with a simple silk wedding dress.

It shaped to her figure and had a high collar in the front. There were no sleeves and the straps at the back dipped low behind her. The bottom had to be her favorite part. It was circular shaped and pooled on the floor around her.

Xiomara and her mother headed out first then her dad took her arm and lead her from the bedroom. As they headed down the stairs, she noticed that the banister was wound with greenery with white flowers and lights. When they reached the bottom and headed down the hall to the backyard where they would have the ceremony, butterflies took off in her stomach.

Pausing at the back door, she got her first glimpse of the transformation. The effort everyone went to for his mating ceremony touched her beyond words. She didn't know most of them very well, yet they did so much for her.

There were hundreds of twinkle lights in the trees, tables set up close to the house and stands with blue hydrangeas set up throughout the area. Araton stood with his brothers in tuxedos. They didn't bother hiding their red wings and they stood out. Araton was the sexiest guy she'd ever seen. It didn't matter if he was wearing leather pants and t-shirts or a tuxedo. He looked good enough to eat.

Araton kissed her mom's cheek and shook her brothers' hands. Seeing them together made joy wash through her.

Glancing up at her dad, she noticed the sheen of tears in his eyes. Lifting to her tiptoes, she kissed his cheek, too then headed out the door. Araton's deep grey eyes met hers and all of the nerves jumping around in her gut settled. This was exactly where she was meant to be. Her entire life led her to the angel she loved.

The Dark Warriors were scattered throughout the backyard along with several other angels. Natalia had met them all over the past few days, but they weren't her friends. Part of her wished more of her friends could have been there, but she knew it was not wise to have more in on the secret. Besides, she hadn't yet decided what she was going to do about her job on the force. That was a worry for another day.

Zakara caught Lia's eye as she fussed with the cupcakes

and other treats near the house. Her mate stood there smiling indulgently at her. It still seemed like a soap opera to her that Kara's mate, Ramiel was married to Elsie, Zander's mate when they were both human.

Shaking those thoughts away, she continued to Araton's side. Lia still felt Lucifer pounding at the edges of her consciousness. He redoubled his efforts at that moment. *Not happening asshole.*

With love in her heart, Lia stopped and took Araton's hand. The instant they touched Raphael stepped forward and lifted his hands gaining everyone's attention. Close to Xiomara, Lia's mother stared at the archangel with wide eyes.

She tried to remember everything Araton told her about the ceremony. Initially, her parents were upset that she wasn't getting married like everyone else. That was a moot point when they said she was being bound by the highest power outside of God himself.

The only reason her father hadn't had a bigger problem with the entire situation was because Araton was an angel. And, also because he was doing it to save her life. Her mother bawled her eyes out when Lia told her she was possessed by Lucifer.

Angels took their places outside the two of them and the Dark Warriors. Wings lifted to surround them. Red, black, blue, gold, purple, and green wings created a gorgeous back-drop. Her family and best friend gazed from the angels around them to Raphael's massive white wings. Yeah, it was overwhelming and humbling to be a part of.

"You definitely have a thing for mating ceremonies, Raphael," Ramiel called out with a chuckle.

Raphael chuckled as well. "Like I said before, uniting a couple in love is one of the best blessings in life. It seems we keep getting blessed with strong females that bring Heaven back to its original glory. I thought we had a better handle on Lucifer after he was freed from the lake, but it seems once again we were missing something. I cannot fathom the strength you possess, Natalia to have fought him off for as long as you have."

Tears shone in her parent's eyes and her dad puffed out his chest. "Our little girl is one of a kind," her dad informed them.

The archangel Michael stepped forward followed by Gabriel. Both clapped her dad on the shoulder. "You're right about that. You both have raised an outstanding daughter," Gabriel told her mom and dad. Natalia was going to start bawling before the ceremony even started.

"Let's get on with this joining," Abraxos murmured, earning a chuckle from the crowd.

"Always impatient, brother," Ayil teased as he kissed Kennex then took a position to the left side of her with Abraxos to the right. Raphael stopped in front of them.

The two Archangels, Gabriel and Michael took positions behind them. She recalled her sister in law, Kennex who she discovered was a freakin' Phoenix, telling her about the five-pointed star they would form with her and Araton in the center. She turned in a circle and watched as the Angels spread their wings, so their tips touched, enclosing them in a colored cocoon of red and white.

The second the wing tips joined Lia heard Lucifer scream in her head. A huge smile spread over her face despite the pain she suffered. She hoped it was a million times worse for the Dark Lord. Energy flowed from them and through her. A second later she felt when the veil Araton told her about snapped into place.

Araton grabbed one of her hands offering comfort as her discomfort grew. She nearly screamed as the energy built around them. The moment each of the Angels surrounding them held out a hand and called a weapon of Light to their palm, her heart raced in her chest and her veins boiled in her body.

While agony seared her from the inside out, she was filled with indescribable love from Araton. In turn, she gritted her teeth against the pain hating that sweat drenched her and allowed her heart to fill with joy, love and adoration.

Raphael extended his weapon above their heads and each Angel touched their Light to his. A flash of white light blasted throughout the sky, sending a jolt right through Lia's body. A scream escaped and Araton wrapped his arms around her shoulders, holding her close.

Holding her gaze, Araton let her see his love and adoration as he murmured, "Fate smacked me over the head with you. From the second I met you, you became my everything. The choice to save you was made before I entered the house and I have never looked back. Our souls joined that night and kept pushing us together. I'm a stubborn fool and ignored it until it nearly cost you your life. I will always love you, Dove. You have me, heart and soul. For eternity."

Tears blurred Lia's vision, as she gazed up at the love of her life. Having an angel like Araton love her made her feel precious and cherished. "I had no idea what I was missing until you flew into my life and saved it. You shine as bright tonight as you did that night and I can't seem to look away. God brought you to me when I needed you most. Without you I would have been lost to Lucifer. I wouldn't change a thing if it meant I wouldn't find you. I love you, Araton. You are my choice."

Araton called his sword of light and touched it to the other angelic weapons above them. Fire shot into the sky creating flaming fireworks. The connection she felt with Araton became a thick, gold ribbon that wrapped around her heart and ran to his. Lucifer shrieked in her mind firing off more demonic energy, trying to sink hooks into her soul. They struck the thick shield Araton erected around her and her pain disappeared along with the Dark Lord.

Her back arched with the strength of the bond she had to Araton. His soul touched hers making her body ignite with need. The urge to strip the tux from his muscular body was nearly undeniable. A flush crept over her cheeks when she realized every supernatural in the backyard would be able to scent her arousal and how much she needed Araton. There was no denying how badly she wanted her angel. How bad would it be to skip the party? She didn't think she could wait.

* * *

ARATON HAD NEVER EXPERIENCED this much joy in his life. And his sister was an angel of joy. His heart now beat for Natalia. The bond to him forced Lucifer to release Lia. The relief of knowing his mate was free from the malicious fallen angel was palpable.

And, now he wanted to take her body. He'd heard stories about what it was like when you mated. Even his brother's description paled in comparison to how deeply the event affected him. Love and need sparked to life the instant his connection with Lia formed. Fervent need for his mate sparked to life from the moment the gold ribbon bound them together. It was something he doubted would ever abate.

Araton brushed her long black hair aside and kissed the side of her neck. His hands roamed up her back and paused at the zipper of her dress. When Lia moaned and grabbed a fist of his hair, he unzipped the silky dress. It fell to the ground leaving her in a strapless bra and satin panties.

Trailing his hands over her stomach and up to her breasts, he listened to make sure they weren't going to be interrupted. Abraxos and several of the Dark Warriors were still downstairs with her best friend Xiomara.

He had no idea who lit the candles in the room, but he made a mental note to thank them later. He recalled tossing rose petals on the floor and lighting candles after Ayil was mated, so he had asked them to make sure he had those elements in their room.

Lia stepped away from him and crawled onto the bed while giving him a hungry look. No need to tell him what she was asking. Araton eagerly crawled after her and hovered over her prone figure when she finally stopped moving.

"You're finally free, Dove. And you're mine. The scent of your arousal after the ceremony was done has been driving me crazy all night," he whispered against her mouth.

Her sparkling green eyes, lush breasts and sweet scent entranced him. And the smile that hadn't left her face for the past three hours was the best part of all. It was one that matched his. His highest priority in life was to make sure that she always smiled like that. And that the lust in her eyes never dimmed a fraction.

"I nearly told my family they could enjoy the food and drinks then drag you up here," she told him with a groan as she tried to lift her hips and rub her core against him.

Araton's mouth went dry when he watched her try to get her pleasure. Spreading her legs, Lia tried to get his shaft to press into her slit. Araton barely stopped his body before it made contact. She lifted her hands and ran them up his sides then lifted her lips to his. Their kiss was instantly explosive and wild.

The energy between them fed the zeal of their need. The electricity arching between their skin made Araton dizzy as he couldn't decide where he needed contact more. Taking matters into her own hands, she unbuttoned his shirt at the same time she slid her tongue inside his mouth.

The erotic rhythm of their kiss made his cock hard as stone.

Allowing the fervor to take over, Araton's mouth devoured hers. Lia arched her back and Araton felt her breasts pop out the top of her bra. Breaking away from her mouth, he lowered his head to suck on her hard nipples.

The bra rode the edge just under her pert nipples and frustrated him at the same time. When he lifted his head and reached behind her, Lia took advantage and unbuttoned his shirt. Her soft hands ran over his chest, making him shiver.

When she pushed the fabric apart, he paused what he was doing to shrug out of the top. Her hands were back on him the second he was back in contact with her skin. He groaned and nearly came in his pants when her fingers teased the top seam of his wings. "Do you like that?"

"God, yes. It feels so fucking good, but it makes it difficult to take this slow," he admitted.

His eyes slipped closed when she teased the top of the insertion where his wings left his body. His big body shuddered, and he went back to licking and sucking her nipples while her fingers played with the sensitive skin, making him greedy.

"Your tongue is pure magic," she purred.

"You like that, love?"

"I never thought it could feel so damn good," she admitted which made him feel a hundred feet tall. "I need you to stop teasing me," Lia panted and lifted her core then pressed it against his shaft.

Reaching between them she fumbled with the button of his pants. Araton pushed her hands aside and pushed her panties down her legs before he tugged them off her legs. Her sweet scent intensified, obliterating everything else.

His fingers roamed between her legs and slid through her arousal. "Torture is having to make nice with your dad while all I want to do is take you to our room and fuck you sense-less. Are you ready for me, Dove?"

Her arousal soaked through the front of his pants and made him lose all semblance of going slow. "More than ready, Wings."

Araton needed to make sure. They hadn't been together many times and she was so tight it nearly hurt. Araton ran his hand up one leg then slid it between their bodies. Her heat scalded his finger as he rubbed her clit in circles.

"Yes. Just like that," she begged.

His mouth lowered to her breast and he sucked, licked and nipped her flesh. Her hips lifted and moved as she rode his hand. She was the sexiest female alive when she took her pleasure. When her arousal flooded his hand, he inserted one finger then another. Scissoring his thick digits, he groaned against her breast when her core clenched. She was close to the edge.

Lifting his head, he claimed her mouth and kissed her passionately while he pumped his fingers in and out of her. The heel of his hand rubbed against her clit. Within seconds her body bowed off the bed and she cried out his name as she detonated.

"I need you to fuck me now," she commanded on a pant.

"Your wish is my command," he told her.

Lia moved fast and gripped the fly of his pants. Her fingers grazed the head of his cock. His skin heated as she kept rubbing over his shaft while she unclasped his pants. Lia had his erection out and in her hot little hand a second later.

She looked between their bodies and licked her lips. It made him want to shove her head down and encourage her to suck his cock in to her hot little mouth. He knew that was going to have to wait for another time but that didn't stop his shaft from jerking in her grip.

He nudged her torso back to the bed. She let go of him

and stared up at him with the most intense heat in her eyes. This gorgeous female was his. They were bound together for eternity. He was still shocked by the turn of events but didn't regret joining with her. He knew his brothers thought it was another rash decision on his part. That couldn't be farther from the truth.

The evidence of how much she wanted him pooled between her legs. The sight made him grab his cock and slide it through her slick folds to coat his length in her arousal. The contact made her hips surge upward. He knew that she wanted him to sink into her heat and it was impossible to stop himself.

"I'll go slow next time," he promised her.

"Fast and hard. Now," Lia demanded.

Araton pressed his lips to hers at the same time he thrust balls deep into her core in one stroke. He nearly lost his seed when she clenched around his cock. That move broke the dam on their mutual need and he settled into a fast, hard rhythm. Pounding into her with each stroke.

Addiction was too tame a word for how much he wanted and needed Lia. His heart pounded in his chest and he had to break away from her lips so they could both breathe. They were both covered in sweat as their bodies moved together.

Reaching between their bodies, he rubbed Lia's clit and pounded in and out of her body, making her buck uncontrollably. Rising onto his knees, he lifted her into his arms so she straddled his lap and she took control. It changed his angle and the head of his shaft kept hitting against her G spot while she rode him. She quickened her pace, chasing after what they both desperately needed.

His finger rubbed her clit harder and before too long he felt her body tense around his cock. It sent his body into overdrive. Pleasure flooded his body while he fought to ensure she came with him. Nothing compared to sex with Lia.

"I choose you to be my mate," he panted as he lifted his hips to meet her downward strokes.

"And, I choose you to be my mate. You are my world, Araton. I love you," she replied. His heart soared and his mouth met hers.

Her love flowed from her and filled his heart a second before she shouted her release and yelled his name. Stars exploded behind his eyes. He was consumed by the need to join her in climax, but he automatically sent his love back to her. A second later his spine tingled, and his balls drew up tight. Araton groaned as his seed exploded from him to fill her up. He wrapped his arms around her and brought her close.

A sense of completion filled him followed by the perfection of their mating. His entire body vibrated with the power of their vow to one another. This ritual was the second part of an angel's mating. There was no force that could separate them now.

Collapsing to the bed and pulling her with him, Araton kissed her forehead and held her close. "Give me five minutes and I'm going to make love to you in the air. I just need a few minutes after you drained me. I love you to Heaven and back."

"To Heaven and back," she agreed and closed her eyes. He held her while she napped thanking God for the gift of his Dove. Life didn't get more perfect.

Thank you for reading this book. If you enjoyed the story, please consider giving me a virtual hug and leaving a review. If this is your first novel of mine, check out my website, www.brendatrim.com, for details on my other works.

I have co-authored over thirty books in the bestselling Dark Warrior Alliance and Hollow Rock Shifters series and am the mastermind behind the Bramble's Edge Academy series, as well as many other titles.

Be sure to sign up for my newsletter so you get the inside scoop and info about exclusive giveaways. You can stalk me on my Facebook page https://www.facebook.com/Author-BrendaTrim for updates and fun information.

Never allow waiting to become a habit. Live your dreams and take risks. Life is happening now.

DREAM BIG!

XOXO,

Brenda

The Dark Warrior Alliance
>Dream Warrior (Dark Warrior Alliance, Book 1)
>Mystik Warrior (Dark Warrior Alliance, Book 2)
>Pema's Storm (Dark Warrior Alliance, Book 3)
>Isis' Betrayal (Dark Warrior Alliance, Book 4)
>Deviant Warrior (Dark Warrior Alliance, Book 5)
>Suvi's Revenge (Dark Warrior Alliance, Book 6)
>Mistletoe & Mayhem (Dark Warrior Alliance, Novella)
>Scarred Warrior (Dark Warrior Alliance, Book 7)
>Heat in the Bayou (Dark Warrior Alliance, Novella, Book 7.5)
>Hellbound Warrior (Dark Warrior Alliance, Book 8)
>Isobel (Dark Warrior Alliance, Book 9)
>Rogue Warrior (Dark Warrior Alliance, Book 10)
>Shattered Warrior (Dark Warrior Alliance, Book 11)
>King of Khoth (Dark Warrior Alliance, Book 12)
>Ice Warrior (Dark Warrior Alliance, Book 13)
>Fire Warrior (Dark Warrior Alliance, Book 14)
>Ramiel (Dark Warrior Alliance, Book 15)

Rivaled Warrior (Dark Warrior Alliance, Book 16)
Dragon Knight of Khoth (Dark Warrior Alliance, Book 17)
Ayil (Dark Warrior Alliance, Book 18)
Guild Master (Dark Alliance Book 19)
Maven Warrior (Dark Alliance Book 20)
Sentinel of Khoth (Dark Alliance Book 21)
Araton (Dark Warrior Alliance Book 22)

Dark Warrior Alliance Boxsets:
Dark Warrior Alliance Boxset Books 1-4
Dark Warrior Alliance Boxset Books 5-8
Dark Warrior Alliance Boxset Books 9-12
Dark Warrior Alliance Boxset Books 13-16

Hollow Rock Shifters:
Captivity, Hollow Rock Shifters Book 1
Safe Haven, Hollow Rock Shifters Book 2
Alpha, Hollow Rock Shifters Book 3
Ravin, Hollow Rock Shifters Book 4
Impeached, Hollow Rock Shifters Book 5
Anarchy Coming Soon

Bramble's Edge Academy:
Unearthing the Fae King
Masking the Fae King
Revealing the Fae King

Midnight Doms:
Her Vampire Bad Boy

Don't miss out!
Click the button below and you can sign up to receive a

FREE copy of Heat in the Bayou plus emails from me about new releases, fantastic giveaways, and my latest laser engraved creation. There's no charge and no obligation.